REVELATION

THE GENESIS MACHINE
BOOK 3

K.J. GILLENWATER

Revelation

ISBN Print: 979-8-9876112-1-0

ISBN eBook: 979-8-9876112-0-3

Cover by Miblart

❀ Created with Vellum

CHAPTER 1

THE C-17 TOUCHED down at Nellis Air Force Base. Charlie stared out the window at the dry desert that stretched out for miles in all directions ending abruptly at some distant brown mountains. Base housing and a golf course stood out in sharp green contrast against the natural surroundings beyond the base's perimeter.

She'd come to grips with her plan during the last hour of the flight. As soon as they arrived at their hotel, she and Orr had agreed to meet and discuss more about what she'd revealed.

Angel's confessions had made her feel closer to him and stoked her attraction for him. What woman wouldn't feel flattered if a handsome man chose her to be his confidante? But now she realized her mistake in keeping his secrets, the truth bubbled up inside. She needed to unburden herself. The sooner, the better.

Gathering their go-bags and stepping out into the early evening sun, the team exited the plane in silence.

Kellerman shielded his eyes and scanned the runway. "I have a work colleague who'll be meeting up with us."

"Work colleague?" Orr made a face.

"Yes, my old boss. I guess he caught wind of the same radar signal." He hefted his bag onto his opposite shoulder. "I don't see him here. He didn't really give me a lot of information."

Strange.

Charlie didn't know Kellerman kept in touch with his previous office. Wouldn't it be difficult with so many levels of security keeping individual research and information compartmented?

"What?" Orr forcefully tucked his shirt into his jeans. "Who are you talking about? Someone from Area 51?"

"Groom Lake," Kellerman corrected.

"How would they know about our radar signal?"

"It's not really *our* radar signal," Charlie offered.

The commander shot her a sharp look.

Kellerman shrugged. "I don't know any more than you do, sir. The professor texted that he'd see me once we'd arrived. I didn't know if he meant Nellis or Lake Havasu. I thought I'd better explain before he showed up. Might look weird."

"You bet it looks 'weird.'" Orr's tone turned harsh. "What kind of work were you doing for this professor?"

The team reached a black Ford Excursion. Wordlessly, Angel opened the back and hefted his bag inside. He took the chief's proffered duffel and did the same. Both men remained silent as the conversation continued.

The entire team knew Area 51 research was rumored to

include extraterrestrial life and UFOs, but nobody said a thing.

"You know I can't talk about that, sir." Kellerman's face turned red. "I thought you should know is all. Sorry I even brought it up."

Orr caught the young lieutenant's arm before he could head to the back of the vehicle. "This is highly irregular. If I find out you leaked information—"

"I didn't leak anything." A sheen of sweat appeared on Kellerman's brow.

Was he nervous or merely overheated? Although the early September desert heat felt hotter than DC, the faint evening breeze seemed to be reducing the outdoor air temperature.

Orr let go of Kellerman and crossed his arms. "Then you'll introduce me to him tomorrow when we drive out to Lake Havasu. I'll ask him personally what turned him on to our radar signal. Let's see what he has to say."

Kellerman gave a curt nod and loaded his bag into the back of the Excursion.

It would be interesting to see how that played out. Charlie had to admit her own curiosity about Kellerman's former boss.

"Sir, where are we staying tonight?" She'd assumed they'd be heading to Lake Havasu upon landing, but his comment had her wondering.

"Don't get too excited, Petty Officer, but we're booked here in Las Vegas."

"Now that's what I'm talking about," Chief Ricard said as he opened the driver's side door. "Who wants to hang with me at the poker tables?" He pointed a finger at Angel, then

Kellerman, noticeably skipping over both her and the commander.

"Calm down, Chief, we're way off the strip." Orr's hackles had settled, and he grinned.

"Vegas is Vegas, sir."

The team climbed into the vehicle and headed off base into the setting sun.

———

Charlie's armpits were sweaty. She had been standing outside Commander Orr's hotel room door for five minutes trying to work up the courage to knock.

Did she really want to tell her boss everything? What if it blew up in her face?

Just as she was about to rap on the door, it flew open.

"Sir!" she choked out.

Commander Orr's eyes widened at the surprise guest. "Petty Officer Cutter. To what do I have the pleasure?"

"Would now be a good time to talk?" After finding her room, she'd changed into more comfortable clothing—a pair of jeans and a sleeveless top.

The commander opened his door in invitation. "Please, come in."

Although a little uncomfortable being alone in her boss's hotel room, they needed privacy for what she was about to tell him.

"Thanks." She rolled her shoulders to loosen the tightness that had settled there. "I'll try to keep this brief."

"Nonsense. I was only heading out to grab a burger." He closed the door and gestured to a loveseat near the window. "I'm not much of a gambler. Vegas is a bit too gaudy for me."

She sat in the proffered seat. "I know what you mean." On her way through the lobby she'd seen no less than three scantily clad Vegas showgirls wearing large feather head-dresses and handing out invitations for a nightly show at a theater down the block. The chief had grinned, Kellerman's ears had reddened, and Angel hadn't even noticed.

"So you mentioned you had more detail on your transla-tions you wanted to share, along with something about Demarco's connection to the pods?" He sat in an office chair, which he had rolled out from under a small desk. "I have to say I was a little surprised when you brought that up." He flashed a quick grin.

"It will make more sense when I explain."

He leaned forward to rest his elbows on his knees. "Please. Explain."

She bit her lip and clasped her hands together. "Special Agent Demarco isn't who you think he is."

The commander's eyebrows shot up.

"I'm not sure if you are aware, but Demarco and I have been—" She cleared her throat.

"Dating?" Orr said. "Yes, I think most of us noticed some-thing had changed between the two of you recently."

Her face heated. Although she thought they'd done a good job of keeping their relationship a secret, clearly that wasn't the case. "Um, yes." She crossed and re-crossed her legs. This was more difficult than she imagined it would be. "As we got to know each other better, he felt comfortable opening up to me. Told me some things about his past."

"Did something happen between you two and now

you're hoping I'm going to punish him for some sort of lover's spat?"

"It's not a lover's spat, sir. I wouldn't be here to discuss something so trivial." This wasn't going well. "It's difficult to explain."

"Maybe get to the point." He glanced at his watch.

She was losing him. In a matter of seconds he'd send her back to her room. "Right. The translations, the research, our office." Where had her determination gone? "The whole reason Demarco wanted to join our team in the first place is because he is one of the people you are looking for."

"What do you mean?" The commander looked perplexed.

"He's a time traveler, sir. He told me so."

He leaned back. "You're joking."

"I'm not joking, sir."

"Angel Demarco is from the fifteenth century? This is ridiculous." His cheeks puffed out as he released a big breath.

"No, sir. That's just it. The translations, the work I've done on them, it lines up with Angel's—Demarco's story. Risa, the woman who wrote the manuscript, who is Armas's mother—Risa is his sister. They are both from the future, sir."

"I don't understand." He rubbed at an eyelid.

"It's true." What if he didn't believe her? "He was worried if anyone found out the truth, he'd be turned into a lab rat."

Charlie explained everything she'd learned about Angel, his origins, the Purists and the Genesis Project, the goals of Byron Allwood, and how his sister fit into everything. She then revealed Angel's view of Allwood's followers—even his own nephew—as impure and against the laws of nature. The commander had been quiet and respectful as she threw out wild details. At any moment, she expected him to laugh and accuse her of playing a joke.

"What else does he know about the pods? Has he explained exactly how he arrived here?" The commander had a pinched expression. "There are so many questions I want answered."

"If he knows what I told you, I don't know what he'd do. He might disappear. He might act on some of his impulses. I'm worried for Armas. I'm not sure what he has in store for him or any other travelers we might encounter."

"His dislike of tech makes a lot of sense now," Orr mused.

Charlie nodded. Was he slowly coming around to the truth? Would he work with her to keep Angel in check and find out as much as they could about the pods and the people inside them?

"Keep this between you and me for now. I need to think through the implications."

She rose from the loveseat. "What will happen to Demarco?"

"Let me worry about that." The commander ushered her to the door. "Be cautious."

She nodded.

"I'll be the one who decides when and to whom to reveal this information." His hand grasped the doorknob. "Your translation work? No more reporting to the team. We'll keep it between you and me. If you must share with Demarco, do it. I don't want him suspecting anything. Otherwise, the chief, the lieutenant, and Petty Officer Storm? Keep them in the dark."

He opened the door.

"Yes, sir." Charlie stepped into the hall.

"Tomorrow at Lake Havasu, let's keep an eye on Demarco. See what he does."

Charlie nodded in agreement, but inside her stomach hardened like a rock.

———

The next morning, the team gathered near the elevators before the two-and-a-half hour drive to Lake Havasu. Charlie stood next to Angel, hoping he'd noticed her change in demeanor. Maybe he'd think their argument was over and everything was back to normal. He didn't seem unhappy she'd approached him.

"Team," said the commander. "We have a bit of a drive this morning, but should be arriving at our destination before noon. I know some of you think we should've pushed on to the location after our flight yesterday, but new information has come to light."

Chief and Kellerman exchanged glances.

Angel touched her hand.

The warmth of his fingers affected her more than she cared to admit.

"I'll share it with you once we're enroute."

The team wended their way from the elevators to the lobby. Even at eight in the morning, gamblers sat on stools in front of clanging and chiming slot machines and drank the free, watered-down drinks from the bar maids. Maybe they should call Vegas the 'city that never sleeps.'

They headed out the automatic doors and into the glaring desert sun.

Brutal.

Charlie held up an arm to block the light. Was the sun brighter in Nevada somehow? Commander Orr donned a pair of sunglasses. Chief pulled his baseball cap lower on his forehead. Demarco and Kellerman squinted.

They all climbed into the waiting black SUV they'd arrived in the night before. Kellerman took the wheel.

As they headed to the highway, Charlie leaned forward to ask the commander a question. "Any update on Armas?"

"Nothing new, I'm afraid. But he's stable, so that's a good sign." Orr slid his sunglasses down his nose to meet her gaze. "Dr. Stern swears she will make sure he pulls through, and if anything changes, she said she'll call. No worries, Petty Officer Cutter, he's in good hands."

Charlie nodded and sat back. She couldn't relax until Armas was out of the woods.

Angel sat next to her, and the chief had selected the back row of seats. Probably because there was a cooler full of drinks and snacks on the floor next to him.

"What's the new information you were going to share, Commander?" asked Demarco.

Orr turned sideways to face the rest of the team. "The pod we're tracking had a pretty rough landing. Instead of hitting the water, which seems typical for the pods, it scraped the top of London Bridge and then skipped across the surface and landed on the shore."

"So a useless trip, then?" Demarco asked.

"Not useless. The local police quickly cordoned off the area after a citizen called it in, and they have someone in custody."

"Someone?" Shivers ran down Charlie's spine. A live

time traveler? She sneaked a peek at Angel who had a furrowed brow and hands closed into fists.

"Man? Woman?" the special agent asked.

"A woman. She was injured, confused, so they took her to the local hospital. They say she's spouting crazy things and think she's got some mental problems."

Orr's gaze locked with Charlie's.

She sucked in her breath.

"So we'll be stopping at the hospital as our first order of business. Lieutenant Kellerman and Chief Ricard, you can drop us off and then head to the crash location to see if you can recover any samples."

"Sir, did they get a name from this woman?" Demarco asked.

Did she detect a tremor in his voice?

"All I know is, she was speaking in gibberish. If she's a time traveler and survived that wreck, she could have some head injuries or otherwise that could be affecting her mind."

Kellerman spoke into his phone to correct their destination on his mapping app. "We're about ninety minutes out, sir."

"Thank you." The commander scanned Demarco's figure for a moment and then turned back around.

The special agent stared out the window, his mind elsewhere.

Charlie scooted closer to him and took one of his hands in hers. Despite her misgivings about his view of the Genesis Project and its followers, she knew what must be running through his mind. "We don't know that it's her," she whispered. "The manuscript only documents one attempt at traveling forward in time."

"Maybe she didn't record everything she did, everything she was thinking." He looked around to make sure no one heard him but Charlie.

"I'll read more of the text. See if there's anything else I can find." It wasn't easy to turn off her sympathetic nature. She couldn't even begin to imagine the pain she'd feel if Chad had disappeared to another time, never to be heard from again.

"Are you still angry with me?" Angel asked with a bitter twinge to his voice.

She shook her head, but her stomach dipped at the lie. "I only want to help, Angel." Until Commander Orr figured out how to handle Angel, she had to stick close to him, make sure he didn't act on his negative feelings toward Allwood's followers.

He smiled briefly and then turned his face toward the window again, as if he wasn't quite certain of her answer.

CHAPTER 2

THE BARE BROWN desert that had surrounded them for two hours changed dramatically as they neared Lake Havasu City. A large swath of deep blue, startling it its size, appeared like a mirage on the horizon. But each mile closer they drove, it became clearer that Lake Havasu was not a mirage, but very real, and very different than the hot, dry country surrounding it.

"The hospital is only a few miles from London Bridge. So close to the crash site," Kellerman said looking down at his phone.

"Keep your eyes on the road, LT," Commander Orr barked from the passenger's seat.

"Yes, sir."

The AI voice on Kellerman's cell directed him to turn away from the bridge and toward the city center. To their right the London Bridge blended almost seamlessly with the modern town built around it. Surprising due to the fact it was almost two hundred years old.

"And where's this professor going to be meeting you?"

Orr asked. He popped a top to a diet soda and took several long sips before setting it in the cup holder between the driver's and passenger's seats.

"He's not meeting me sir." Kellerman checked his mirrors and changed lanes. "He happened to be coming to the same coordinates based on his own research."

"Right. You said something similar yesterday." Orr's tone indicated doubt. "Has he contacted you today?"

"No, sir."

Orr stretched his legs out. "And you won't be sharing with him any additional details, such as the possibility of a crash survivor?"

"I would never break my oath, sir." The lieutenant gave a quick sideways glance at his commanding officer.

"Never?"

Kellerman's neck turned bright red. "No, sir. I'm offended you think you have to ask me, sir."

"I have to protect the integrity of this group. My job is to ensure security and that includes the details of our investigations. It seems as if you look up to this professor, and maybe want to impress him." Orr turned in his seat. "Chief, you stick to the LT like glue. You hear me? Nobody tells anyone anything about why we're here and what we're investigating."

"Yep, Commander, you got it." Chief choked out from a mouth full of potato chips.

Clearly, he'd found the snacks in the cooler.

"I don't need Chief babysitting me, sir." Kellerman stiffened in the driver's seat.

"Don't think of it as babysitting," Orr said. "Think of it as my insurance policy that you aren't going to fuck up our investigation."

Chief's booming laugh filled the SUV. "I'll keep an eye on him, sir. Keep the baby in the playpen."

Charlie observed Kellerman's profile. His eyebrows lowered over his eyes and, if she looked hard enough, she thought she could see steam coming out of his ears.

"Shut. Up. Chief," Kellerman ground out between his teeth.

Chief snorted, unfazed by the lieutenant's temper flare.

The SUV made a sharp turn to the left. All the passengers, with the exception of Kellerman, grabbed onto whatever they could to maintain their seats. He bounced them into the hospital parking lot. "Here we are."

The vehicle ground to an abrupt halt sending all the passengers forward.

"Thank you, LT." Orr clapped Kellerman on the shoulder and then grabbed his soda. "I'll text you when we're ready for a pick-up."

After Charlie and Angel slid out of the Excursion, Kellerman took off in a squeal of tires.

She wasn't so sure it was a good idea to piss off Kellerman. Who knew what his relationship was with this mysterious professor? Maybe he'd leak details out of spite for the way Chief and Orr had treated him.

A bad feeling entered her bones as they stepped through the entrance of the hospital.

———

Angel and Charlie stood in the waiting area while the commander spoke with the reception desk about locating the room of the crash survivor. Orr flashed his NCIS badge, and the young woman at the desk widened her eyes, picked up a phone, and pressed a number.

"I think she'll cooperate," Angel said with a smile.

"Do you think the time traveler will be someone you know?"

His face clouded. "I'm not sure."

"You never did explain how you ended up in a pod." Charlie couldn't help it. She needed to know, needed to understand. If he hated everything about the Genesis Project, why would he have willingly set foot into one of them?

Angel shifted his gaze. "This isn't really the place for such a conversation," he whispered.

"I want to understand everything." She touched his arm.

He brushed off her hand. "Let's talk more when we go home."

"At your place?" Her stomach clenched at the deceit, but she knew he'd accept. Their physical connection had been very strong from the beginning. For now, she had to fake her feelings. She'd find a way to back out of it before they returned to D.C.

His gaze searched her face. "Yes. My place."

"Let's go you two." The commander gestured for them to join him. "We have an escort coming. She's on a secure wing."

They followed their boss as he led them to the elevators.

A nurse dressed in purple scrubs joined them. "Are you the group from the government?"

"Yes, we're here to talk to the accident survivor," Orr said.

She nodded. "How many government organizations are they going to send?"

"Excuse me?"

"There's someone else talking to her right now. Don't you guys share notes?"

The elevator opened, and the four of them stepped inside. The nurse waved her badge in front of a reader and pressed the fifth floor button.

"What are you talking about? What 'someone else'?" Orr crossed his arms.

The nurse frowned and glanced at each of them, as if looking for an answer. "Didn't they tell you downstairs? That's why I was so confused. We already have a government authority here questioning her. Now you guys, too? She's not a well woman. The doc wants her to have some rest. All of these people trooping in and out? Not good for someone with a mental health issue."

"What government authority?" Angel tugged at his tightly tucked shirt.

The elevator stopped at the fifth floor. The door opened.

"A professor somebody-or-other. I can't remember his name. From some Air Force base in Nevada." The nurse exited the elevator and led them down the hall. "This way, please."

The three A Group representatives exchanged glances, then followed the nurse.

"Do you think that's Kellerman's professor?" asked Charlie.

"Guess we don't have to worry about Kellerman spilling the beans to him at the crash site," Angel said.

"I don't like this." The commander picked up his stride.

The nurse waved her badge in front of a card reader on

the patient room door. The door beeped. She opened it. "You have ten minutes. Doctor's orders."

A tall man wearing a crisp gray suit and rimless glasses exited from the men's restroom and passed them in the hall. He nodded at them. When he noticed Angel, his mouth opened slightly and his eyes became steely.

"Allwood?" Angel whispered and turned his head as the man walked by.

Charlie grabbed his arm. "Hey."

Orr had entered the room, and the nurse waited for the two of them to join him.

The tall man picked up his pace and continued down the hall without a word.

"Was that the other government authority you were talking about?" Angel demanded. "The professor? Byron Allwood!" He shook himself free of Charlie's grasp and chased the man down the hall. "Stop!"

"Angel, what are you doing?"

He'd run off after the stranger.

"That's right. Professor Allwood." The nurse replied, as if nothing was wrong with Angel chasing this man through the hospital. "Do you know him?" She gave Charlie a quizzical look.

"Petty Officer Cutter, let's go." Orr beckoned her inside the patient room.

Beyond the door she could see a pale woman lying in the hospital bed wearing restraints. "But sir, Demarco, he—"

"Where is he?" Orr appeared in the doorway.

"He ran off after the professor. He thinks it's Byron Allwood."

"It *is* Byron Allwood," said the nurse.

Charlie's thoughts scrambled to understand. "What should we do?" She didn't know what Angel had in mind for the man he'd hated all of these years. Was Kellerman's former boss the infamous Byron Allwood? How was that possible?

Orr looked down the hall. "Shit." He let out a sigh. "You stay with the patient. I'll take care of this."

Charlie entered the room, her heartbeat racing. Stars filled her vision. To comprehend what was happening took her breath away. How could she focus on the woman lying in the bed when two mortal enemies had crossed paths? What did it mean for Armas? For the team? For Angel?

———

"Byron is that you?" the woman in the bed called out weakly.

Charlie wanted to be out in the hallway with her boss, Angel, and the mysterious Allwood. Not here in the room with a pod crash survivor. She was inconsequential compared to what was happening outside of this room. But her boss had wanted her to meet with the woman, so she would follow orders. "My name is Petty Officer Cutter, I'm from NCIS-A. Did the nurse tell you? We'd like to ask you some questions."

She really didn't have any questions in mind. She'd assumed Orr would take the lead on the conversation, but now that she was alone with her, maybe she could find some of her own answers.

"Where is Byron? He told us we would all be together again." The patient pulled at her restraints. "Where am I?"

Charlie pulled up a chair. "You're in the hospital."

The woman, who was barely out of her teens, had long brown hair, a cherub face, and a snub nose. She turned her head in Charlie's direction. "Are we in paradise?"

"Excuse me?"

The woman blinked. One eye was milky blue, the other a dark brown.

Charlie gasped at the odd appearance.

A large jagged scar was visible down the side of her face from scalp to chin. The woman reached for her hand. "Paradise. He told us we were traveling to paradise. A world without hate and fear."

Charlie clasped the woman's hand in hers. "You are in a safe place. They will take care of you here, I promise. What's your name?"

"Safe. Yes, I want to be safe."

The woman's grip tightened like a vise.

"Ow, you're hurting me." Charlie twisted her arm to break the woman's hold.

"I don't know you. Who are you? Why should I trust you?" The woman's face twisted into a snarl. The soft, child-like features disappeared.

"I want to help you." Charlie managed to free her hand. "Tell me your name, so I can help you."

"You think I haven't seen your tricks? The tricks of the Purists?"

"I'm not here to hurt you."

"Is that right? The last time I saw your kind, I was being chased through the tunnels, attacked for being different, I would've died if it weren't for Risa and Byron." She struggled against her restraints. "They saved us—the most loyal, the most obedient—we were rewarded. I am here in paradise like I was promised."

"This isn't paradise."

"Where is Byron?"

"You traveled through time. You're in the past. The world as it is now is probably no better than the time you came from. We have violence and problems and everything else. Allwood lied to you."

The woman bucked upward. "No! You're a liar. You're Purist scum."

The nurse entered the room. "I'm sorry, your time is up." She fluttered around the agitated patient and adjusted the blankets. "You're safe here, remember? Nothing can hurt you here."

The woman began to relax with the nurse's ministrations and soothing words.

"Did she give you a name?" As she asked the nurse the question, Charlie moved her chair back where she found it by the window.

"No. But she did seem to know that professor your friend chased after." The nurse checked the patient's IV line. "We're hoping we can track down her family, but she didn't have any ID on her."

Suddenly, the patient grabbed at her throat. Her eyes grew wide and panicked.

The nurse rushed to the woman to check her pulse. "What have you done?"

"Nothing." Charlie backed away from the bed. "I only was asking her questions."

The woman's face turned purple.

"She's not breathing." The nurse pushed a button on the

control attached to the patient's bed. Then, she quickly released the rail on the side of the bed and removed the pillow from beneath the woman's head. "What did you do?"

Charlie shook her head and skirted the end of the bed, heading for the door. Where was the commander? She shouldn't be in here.

Another nurse burst through the doorway with a crash cart. A doctor seconds behind.

As the team circled the unresponsive patient, Charlie slipped out into the hall. Would she be okay? The woman had seemed perfectly lucid and awake when she'd entered the room. Maybe an undiagnosed injury from the crash? Or her time travel experience?

She reflected on the survivor's appearance—her eyes, the long scar down her face. Maybe Angel was right. Had Allwood been experimenting on innocent people? And what was Allwood's purpose in doing so? Maybe Angel's anger was reasonable. Seeing the crazed woman for herself had given her a different perspective. Was Allwood a caring man who wanted to advance humans for the better? Or some kind of Dr. Frankenstein?

"We're losing her—"

Charlie's stomach dropped.

CHAPTER 3

ANGEL RACED DOWN THE HALLWAY. He couldn't let Allwood slip away. The knowledge that Allwood had been Kellerman's boss at Area 51 made his stomach turn. What kinds of experiments had they let him get away with? And how did he end up working for them anyway?

A nurse stepped into his path. He dodged and spun bouncing off the wall. The woman gasped and reared back. He missed colliding with her by inches.

Allwood sprinted ahead of him. A few more feet, and he would reach the bank of elevators at the end of the hall.

Angel felt for the gun he'd tucked in the back of his pants under his jacket. No one on the team had known he was armed. Even though he held the role of 'security,' the commander discouraged Angel from carrying any weapons. But when Angel heard on the ride to Lake Havasu they had a pod survivor, he was glad he'd done it.

"Allwood!" He was closing the distance.

The older man stumbled, but he caught himself, gripping the wall as he turned a corner—not toward the elevators but following a sign for the stairs.

How many years had Allwood been here? The last time Angel had seen him, he was still a young man. No more than thirty. Now he looked well into middle age—bald, a bit of a paunch, and an uneven gait. Twenty years? Maybe more? The chief's data indicated a pod had landed in the late nineties. Perhaps that had been Allwood's pod.

He rounded the corner. The older man pushed through the stairwell door. Angel was mere steps behind. As he burst through it seconds after Allwood, he took a chance and leapt at his prey. Angel crashed into him as he headed downstairs. Their bodies collided. They tumbled together down the stairs to the landing, and Angel had the air knocked out of him. His gun flew out of his hands and bounced off the wall. They both landed with a hard thud.

Allwood groaned. He'd hit his head on one of the steps and bled freely from a cut on his scalp. Angel balled up his fist and pounded the man in the face. The older man crossed his arms to protect himself from the hail of blows. Over and over Angel punched the man. His mind was a single thought: kill him.

Somehow the smack of his fist against Allwood's chin satisfied a deep seated need in him. A need to punish. A need to destroy. A need to end this man's life right here, right now before he harmed anyone else.

"Demarco!" The commander's voice echoed in the stairwell. "Get the fuck off that man. What in the hell do you think you're doing?" Within seconds, his boss had reached the pair of scuffling men and had Demarco in a headlock.

Orr hauled Demarco off Allwood. Angel was surprised

how strong the commander was. He fought him with every-thing he had, but the choking hold diminished his strength quickly.

Allwood scrambled away from both of them and scooped up the gun.

When Orr saw the weapon, he loosened his grip on Demarco.

"Shit." Angel spat on the tile, hauled himself up, and hurtled toward the now-armed Allwood and barreled into the man with his shoulder.

The gun went off, and a bullet glanced off the stairs above them and buried itself in the tile floor right in front of Orr.

Angel latched onto Allwood's arm with both hands in a struggle for the weapon. "Drop it, Allwood."

Their faces were inches apart. The jagged scar he'd remembered on Allwood's face had faded to a faint white line. "What did you do to her?" the older man asked.

"What did I do to her?" Angel pulled back slightly. His mind raced.

"The pod survivor is just fine," Orr said as he plucked the gun out of Allwood's restrained hand. "I don't know what's going on here." He nodded at Allwood. "But one of you better start talking."

Orr's cell phone rang. He pressed his lips together, looked at the phone screen, sighed, and answered it. "Petty Officer Cutter, this had better be important." As he listened, the commander's face paled.

———

Charlie hung up the phone and leaned against the wall next to the patient room where the pod survivor had died. The host of nurses and doctors who had poured in to save the woman's life had failed. Now A Group would never know more about the time she came from, why she'd willingly gotten into a pod, or how many more of these travelers existed.

The nurse, who had been in the room with Charlie when the patient coded, warned her not to leave, as the doctor would want to speak with her. Why did the nurse think she had something to do with the woman's sudden change in condition? She wiped her sweaty palms on the front of her pants. She needed her boss to step in and fix this. Something wasn't right.

But Orr had sounded breathless on the phone. Had Angel caught up to Allwood? Had Orr managed to stop them both from killing each other? Maybe the commander had his hands full.

"Young lady?" A short Asian man in a doctor's coat approached her. "Are you the one who was with the patient earlier?"

She nodded. "My name is Charlie Cutter. I'm with the government. We were sent here to investigate a crash by the lake. The woman was our witness." She opened her purse and pulled out one of the generic looking business cards Stormy had given her last week.

The doctor took the card and read the face of it. "You're Navy?"

"Yes."

His face softened. "My dad was a Navy Flight Officer. Did twenty-five years. I almost went to the Naval Academy."

Charlie smiled.

"I'm Dr. Phan."

They shook hands.

"What happened to her?" Charlie nodded toward the patient room. "She was totally fine when I first went in there, but then after the nurse arrived—"

He nodded and tapped his pen against his cheek. "The nurse mentioned another visitor before you. Was he part of your investigative team?"

She shook her head. "I was here with my boss, Commander Orr, and another co-worker, Special Agent Demarco. If you know anything about another visitor, we could really use some more information."

The doctor's eyebrows shot up. "I only know there were two requests today for visitors. I gave the okay, as long as they were brief visits. I was hoping someone would be able to help us identify her, and when I heard you were from the government, well, I hoped you knew something we didn't."

"I'm sorry. I can't give you any details about our investigation. I'm sure you understand."

The doctor nodded, but Charlie wasn't certain he truly understood.

"I only wish I knew what happened in there," he said.

"Oh? I thought maybe she had an injury from the crash."

"We did a thorough exam last night when she was admitted—CT, x-rays, blood work. The scans all came back normal. We're still waiting on the blood results. But what we saw in there...well, it almost seems as if—" He trailed off and shrugged.

"As if what?"

"As if she was injected with something. Her condition deteriorated so rapidly."

The hair lifted on the back of her scalp. Had Allwood done something to the woman? The leader of the Genesis Project and supposed 'savior' who brought the survivor to 'paradise'?

Her mind flitted through the possibilities. She'd assumed Allwood had shown up at the hospital to rescue one of his followers, but now it looked as if he was taking her out. Why?

"Dr. Phan, my team will have to take possession of the blood and the results. Can you show me where I can retrieve those?"

"What?" The tapping of his pen against his cheek ceased. "I can't approve that."

"And the body. We'll need to have the body ready to be transported by the end of today." Orr had instructed her very carefully about what she needed to do. Would the doctor listen to her?

"Excuse me, but we have protocols here." Dr. Phan tucked his pen into the breast pocket of his white coat. "An autopsy must be performed, so we can identify cause of death, make sure no foul play was involved."

"Doctor," a familiar voice said, "I'm sorry but this is now a federal case." Commander Orr approached flashing his A Group badge. "We'd appreciate your cooperation."

Charlie bit her lip. "Where's Demarco?" *And Allwood,* she thought.

Her boss let out a sigh. "That's a long story. Let's go pick up the blood work and arrange for the body to be delivered to Nellis, and I'll catch you up."

The doctor stood between them and rubbed at his eyelid.

Orr clapped him on the shoulder. "Thanks, doc, you've been helpful."

———

Allwood, zip cuffs restraining his hands, attempted to stand in the ER waiting room. "You can't keep me here. I'm not a criminal."

Angel grabbed him by the belt and forced him to sit.

A middle-aged nurse with a tired look on her face approached them with a clipboard. "Calm down, sir, I'm sure the officer only wants you to be treated for your injuries."

"He's not an officer." The older man's lip curled. "He's unlawfully restraining me."

Angel flashed his NCIS-A badge. "I'm with the Naval Criminal Investigative Service. He's my detainee and is wanted for questioning. Could you please clean him up, maybe give him a few stitches?"

Allwood jerked his head back when he saw the badge. "How did you manage that one?"

"Same as you managed to convince people you were a professor."

The nurse inspected his head wound and the bruising to his face. "Did you have an accident?"

"This thug tackled me in the stairwell and punched me." Allwood's face reddened. "I want you to call the police."

Angel made eye contact with the nurse and gave a slight shake to his head.

"Let's examine you first and take care of that cut," the

nurse soothed. "Then we can decide what to do next. All right?"

Allwood calmed down, and his posture relaxed. "Yes, thank you. At least someone here is listening to me." He announced it to the room as if the other people waiting for emergency medical care had any interest in his situation.

The nurse handed Angel the clipboard. "Please fill in his information for him and any insurance provider."

"I'm not paying for this," Allwood squawked.

"We'll be paying cash," Angel explained as he filled out the form.

"You can bring it with you." The nurse took hold of Allwood's arm. "Come this way. We've got a room for you to wait in. The doctor will be with you shortly."

Although the man towered over the portly nurse, he let himself be led as if he were a small child. Allwood was shifty —pathetic one minute, brutal the next.

Angel's mind veered back to his sister, what had she been thinking when she joined the Genesis Project? And how had she ended up with this rat?

————

The 'room' was a curtained off area near the back of the emergency department. Angel took the only chair and filled out the form. "I know your name, but what's your address? And how old are you these days, Byron?"

He held the pen over the form and eyed his captive who comfortably lay on the gurney, dried blood marring his brow and a bruise darkening on his chin.

"You think I'm going to give you my address?" Allwood sneered.

"Yes, I do. Because if you won't give it to me, I'll be forced to call the officer in charge back at Area 51 and ask him for your details."

"Groom Lake. Only civilians call it that." He pulled down his jacket sleeve with his handcuffed hands.

Angel slammed the clipboard on the counter next to him. "Enough of this shit, Allwood." He lowered his voice so it wouldn't carry beyond the curtains surrounding them. "I never thought I do it, but I found you. And now your whole scheme is over with."

"What whole scheme exactly?" He crossed his ankles and put his restrained hands behind his head in a relaxed pose.

"The pods, the traveling, your followers. It's over." He leaned toward the older man. "I don't know what you're up to, but it ends here. Today. No more of your sick experiments."

"Aren't we looking for the same thing, Demarco? Haven't we always been since we arrived here?"

His pulse increased. Was Allwood about to reveal some of his secrets? "I don't know what you're talking about."

"Yes, you do." The professor tilted his head from side to side until his neck cracked. "You couldn't stand to let Risa make up her own mind. Choose her own path. She told me about you, you know."

"Shut up." Angel ground his teeth together.

"How you despised her intelligence. Was embarrassed by her. How you never stood up for her."

"That's not true," Angel snorted. "I protected her. My father—"

"Your father. Yes, tell me more about the man who made her life a living hell." Allwood raised an eyebrow. "Squashing her brilliance. Forcing her to live the life of a farmer's daughter."

"She loved our family." A heaviness filled his body. Had Risa really told him that? Had she despised their simple way of living?

Allwood smirked. "If she loved her family so much, why did she seek me out?"

"You're wrong, Allwood." He crossed his arms. All these years of waiting to confront the man who took his sister away and now he was in a battle of words. He had questions he wanted answered, but found himself distracted by strong emotion. "You took advantage of her. She was a young girl. She didn't know what she was doing. You lied to her."

"She was twenty and perfectly capable of making up her own mind." He casually touched his wound with his fingers and looked at the bright red blood on them. "Don't you think?"

A pain hit the back of his throat. "You killed her, and I'll never forgive you for that."

CHAPTER 4

ALLWOOD'S FACE PALED. "What do know about her?"

Angel's body tensed. "You put her in one of those pods, and sent her back to the dark ages. That's what I know. I'm sure you've seen the manuscript. It's your fault."

"You stupid fool." Spots of color entered the older man's cheeks. "You have no idea what part you played, do you? Why I ended up separated from her?" He frowned. "Why didn't you let us leave? We weren't hurting anyone."

"Hurting anyone?" Just as he remembered, Allwood was an arrogant prick who didn't give a fuck about anyone but himself. "You were surgically altering vulnerable people. Promising them cures and a better life. I saw what your 'treatments' did to people." A sour taste filled his mouth.

"They chose that path. I didn't make them do it."

"You made ridiculous promises that were never going to be real," Angel spat out. "You took life and ruined it. You ruined her—Risa."

Allwood gaze became unfocused. "She was even more

beautiful after I helped her become the person she was supposed to be."

"A monster?"

Allwood snorted and shook his head. "I made her better, smarter. I helped her fulfill her true purpose, her true destiny."

"To die alone in some barbaric time?" Blood pounded in his ears. "Where women were burned at the stake for witchcraft?"

"You were the one who sent her there, Demarco. When you damaged her pod. It was your fault and yours alone. We only wanted to escape where our work could be understood."

How dare Allwood blame him? "Is that what's happening now at Groom Lake? Continuing your work?"

The curtain flew open, and a woman in a white coat entered. "I've heard you need some stitches, Mr. Allwood. I'm Doctor Sala."

Angel found himself standing over Allwood in an aggressive stance. The doctor's arrival made him turn off his anger and resume the role of arresting authority. "I have a transport arriving in a few minutes. Will this take long?"

Dr. Sala approached the patient, donned a clean pair of gloves, and examined the wound. "I'd guess about ten stitches. That's quite a cut. Would you like an ice pack for the bruising?"

"Yes, thank you," said Allwood. "At least someone cares about my injuries."

Angel wanted to punch his bruised face a few more times.

"It shouldn't take more than twenty minutes." The doctor

turned her attention back to the patient. "Let's get you all patched up, shall we?"

————

As Angel watched Dr. Sala stitch up Allwood, he reviewed the facts of what he knew. Allwood and Risa had attempted to escape to the past using pods, which according to Charlie's translation work, had been the scientific work of his sister. And even though Allwood's followers had joined him, Angel was beginning to wonder if that had merely been a way for the two lovers to cover their tracks. What was the true purpose of the pods? To allow the Genesis Project to continue in another time? Or was it a more personal pursuit? What made his sister want to create such a thing?

Even though he thought he understood Risa—after all they were only eighteen months apart in age—had he missed something? He recalled fondly their childhood together on the farm, spending time in the barn with the animals and playing in the hay stacks up in the loft. Yes, she had struggled with the expectations of her family and the community, but he never thought her unhappy.

For Angel, the jump to the past had been a startling one. Something he hadn't anticipated. The sensation of floating and spinning had been odd. He had imagined himself traveling through the air to another part of the earth, and, he had to admit, deep down he found that exciting. He'd lived his whole life in his little village with the same people, the same work, the same future laid out in front of him. But when he'd made the decision to step into the pod and follow his sister, had he been choosing that to rescue her or to save himself?

"There, all done." The doctor wiped away the dried blood and studied her handiwork. "It should heal well and will barely be visible." She touched Allwood's scar that marred the side of his face. "Have you ever thought about plastic surgery for that? Not sure what happened here, but it must've not been a very skilled hand."

Allwood jerked his head away

The doctor lowered her hand. "I'm sorry. I didn't mean to—"

Angel handed her the clipboard. "I told the nurse we'll be paying cash. Is there somewhere where I go to do that?"

The doctor took it and flipped through the pages. "We'll need an address on here, so our accounting department can send you a bill."

Angel pulled a business card out of his shirt pocket. "You can send it here."

The doctor frowned. "Washington D.C.?"

"Come on. Let's go." He hauled up the older man by his elbow.

"He needs his anti-biotics." Dr. Sala slid back the curtain. "The hospital pharmacy is down the hall on the first floor. The prescription should be ready by now."

Angel's phone rang. While holding onto Allwood with one hand, he dug his cell phone out of his pocket with the other. "Hello?"

The doctor handed Allwood a slip of paper with instructions on it and headed to the patient next to them behind another curtain.

"The pod survivor is dead," the commander said on the other end of the line. "We think Allwood might've given her something. Be careful."

"Got it." Angel eyed the man next to him.

"We're down at the lab collecting her blood samples and test paper work. First floor."

Angel processed the possibility that Allwood had murdered one of his supposed followers. Why would he want to do that? "We have to pick up some medication and then we can meet you there."

"Everything okay?"

"I have it under control." Angel tightened his hold on his captive.

"Wonder what the LT's going to think."

"I don't know, but I think Kellerman has some questions to answer.

CHAPTER 5

Back at Walter Reed....

DR. STERN RUBBED HER EYES. It had been a long and uncomfortable night sleeping on the cot in the hospital staff lounge, but she hadn't wanted to leave Armas's side until his vitals improved. Only when the night nurse insisted she leave the ICU and get some rest, did the doctor give in to advice.

As she sat on the edge of the cot, she straightened her blouse and slipped on her navy flats. Since no one had called or texted last night, it must mean Armas was still stable.

She wanted to take a moment and let the good news settle in. Yesterday had been touch and go—she hadn't shared with Charlie how close Armas had been to death. The young petty officer had grown so attached to the child in such a short period of time, she couldn't crush her hopes. Plus, Stormy would've fallen apart. Tetanus at this stage even with modern medicine had a low survivability rate. It had been a difficult decision to withhold the facts about Armas, but the team had work to do. More important work than sitting around a hospital while a little boy struggled to survive.

Her cell phone rang. When she picked it up, a fluttery feeling hit her stomach.

Her contact at the NSA lab.

That could mean only one thing...

"Hello, Sam. Do you have news for me?" she asked.

"Good afternoon." The familiar grizzled voice of her old mentor made her smile. "I hope you're not eating your lunch."

She checked her watch, twelve-thirty p.m. She'd slept longer than she'd thought. "No, not at all." She cleared her throat.

"Probably not the news you were expecting."

"Oh?" Goose bumps appeared on her arms. As her brain ran through the possibilities, she rubbed her forearm.

"The elimination DNA you sent."

Her posture perked up. "Just spit it out, Sam." That was Charlie's sample. The one to make sure her DNA didn't mix in with the DNA from the blood on the broken test tubes the team brought back from North Dakota.

"We got a hit."

"What do you mean?"

"A match."

"To what?" Dr. Stern's mind raced. What was Sam talking about?

"The DNA sample you turned in a week later. They're related."

Armas's sample from the night of his arrival? What was going on?

Dr. Stern held her hand against her mouth. "Related how?" Her heart beat a million miles a minute.

"Half-siblings. Different mitochondrial DNA, but similar paternal strands."

Armas and Charlie were half-brother and sister? But how...? "I see." It was nearly impossible to remain calm. This news had massive implications. It made no sense and called into question everything she'd thought she knew about the young woman she'd grown to respect and appreciate.

"And there's more."

"More?" She stared straight out in front of herself, not seeing the room around her. It was as if the walls disappeared, the cots, the curtains, the chair in the corner. A sleepy-looking young intern stumbled into the dimly lit room and grabbed a cot next to her and pulled the curtain shut.

Dr. Stern picked up her cardigan draped across her lap and exited the lounge. Where could she find some privacy?

"On all three samples you sent us, the DNA swabs plus the blood, we saw some identical cellular-level damage."

The same damage she had noticed on the samples Kellerman retrieved on his recent trip to North Dakota? The damage she'd ascribed to time travel? "Did you send the report to NCIS-A?" She needed to compare her results to the lab's.

"I was about to hit send on my email. You were copied on it."

Suddenly, a gaggle of young privates with fresh haircuts and baby faces filled the hall. Their chatter bounced off the hard flooring and surfaces making it hard to hear Sam on the other end of the line.

Dr. Stern stuck a finger in her ear before responding to

block out the noise. "Can you give me an hour before you do that?"

The group passed by her laughing at some raunchy joke one of the men shared with his buddies. The smallest of them met her gaze and blushed bright red at the possibility they'd been overheard.

"Is there a problem?" Sam asked.

"No, no problem." She took a deep breath to control the shakiness in her voice. "I need to make a phone call first."

"I suppose I could do that for you, Abigail."

"I appreciate it, Sam." Thank goodness she'd sent the samples to the classified lab where she had a contact. The results would go no further than the SCIF at the National Security Agency. But the copy of the report sent to NCIS-A? The explosive information in that report could shatter the trust that had been built among the team. "You'll destroy the samples, yes?"

"Of course."

"Thanks for everything."

Dr. Stern hung up and thought for a moment before selecting a saved number in her contacts list. A familiar voice on the other end amped up her nerves. "We need to talk. Are you free?"

CHAPTER 6

CHARLIE STOOD next to Commander Orr waiting for the hospital lab to hand over the blood and other samples they took from the time traveler along with her CT scan and x-rays. The body had already been loaded into an ambulance and would be delivered to Nellis for the return flight to DC in a couple of hours.

Orr pounded on the bullet-proof glass that protected the lab staff from any threat that might enter their domain. "Where are my samples? Hello?" Little did they know Orr was more dangerous than any threat they could've imagined. He was on the warpath.

Two white-coated lab techs, one male and one female, whooshed past the counter and disappeared into a lab area protected by a security door. Neither one of them seemed interested in dealing with the irate Navy man with the bulging biceps and a bone to pick.

"This is ridiculous. We have to go back tonight. We don't have time for this shit." He threw up his hands and faced

Charlie. "Have you heard anything from Chief or Kellerman?"

"No, sir." By now she understood Orr had serious misgivings about Kellerman's relationship to Allwood. "What about Demarco and Allwood? What did he tell you?"

Orr chewed on his lip before answering. "Sounds as if Allwood was stitched up, and they'll be joining us here in a few minutes."

"How are you going to handle this, sir?"

"If Allwood killed the survivor, we have some serious questions to ask him. I'm not even going to think about what you told me earlier. That's a whole different ball of wax." He ran a hand through his short hair. "But the fact that the professor came here on behalf of Area 51 could pose some problems."

"How?"

"I'm sort of familiar with the structure at the base. Allwood should be under the purview of the base commander and possibly a division chief. They might be expecting his return with samples or even the woman's body. If we interfere, I'm not certain we'd get very far."

"May I help you?" A brave lab worker stood behind the counter. She must've not gotten the message from the other lab techs about Orr's threatening behavior.

The commander pasted a smile on his face and approached the protected space. "I would like to pick up Jane Doe's samples and test results, please. Commander Orr. NCIS." He slid a card through the narrow space under the bullet-proof glass. "Jane Doe from the fifth floor."

The tech's eyes widened. "Right, yes. Dr. Phan's patient."

At that moment Charlie's phone rang. She looked at the

screen. "It's Dr. Stern, Commander. Perhaps she had news about Armas." Her heart thudded. Was the boy all right?

He waved a hand at her, more intent on ensuring they left the hospital with the records he wanted.

Charlie stepped out into the hall where it was quieter. "Abigail, is Armas okay?"

"Listen to me carefully, Charlie."

The serious tone in Dr. Stern's voice worried her. She placed a hand on the wall next to her for support. "I'm listening."

"A report will be delivered shortly to the NCIS-A office. One that has results your co-workers might find shocking."

"What report?" She rubbed her forehead. "What are you talking about?"

"Charlie, I really like you, I do. I'm only letting you know what I found out because I want to understand what's going on. I can't believe you'd lie to me—"

"Lie to you?" Did Dr. Stern know about Demarco and his past? Her blood chilled.

"The lab at NSA called me a few minutes ago. They completed the DNA testing on the blood sample from North Dakota and the testing on Armas." She paused. "I know."

"I don't understand." Her body heat started to rise. "What do you know?"

"I know you and Armas are half-brother and sister."

A roar filled her ears, and her limbs began to shake. "What?" Impossible. There must be some mistake. The lab must've screwed up. There was no way...no possible way...

"Are you a time traveler, too, Charlie? Is that how you ended up on the team? Is that why you were so easily able to translate the manuscript text? Help me understand."

Her grip on her cell phone tightened. How could she and Armas be brother and sister? She had a mother and father who had a house in Columbia and had been married for over two decades. Her only sibling was Chad, her twin. This was madness. "The tests are wrong. I don't know what's going on, but it's not true."

"My friend at the lab wouldn't make that kind of mistake, Charlie."

"It *is* a mistake." A lump formed in her throat. What else could it be? "What you're saying is impossible."

"As soon as you arrive back in DC, the rest of your team will know. You might want to think about trusting me and telling me the truth. I can help you."

Down the hall, Demarco and Allwood in plastic cuffs appeared. Angel's gaze captured hers. A strange feeling ran through her.

"I have to go." The DNA results made no sense, but even if it didn't make sense, the doctor was right—her whole team was about to find out, including Demarco. Her eyelids fluttered. "I'll call you back when I'm free." She felt detached from her body. How could this be? How could such a mistake be made? She needed to know more, needed to talk to the doctor in private, needed to see the results for herself.

CHAPTER 7

"WHO WAS THAT?" Demarco asked as he approached with his captive.

Charlie slipped her phone into her purse and waved a hand. "It's my brother." As she said the words, it dawned on her that Dr. Stern's reveal connected to her twin brother as well. If she was flagged in that report, her brother would be connected as well—it would only be a matter of time. She chewed on her bottom lip.

Her gaze flicked over to Allwood. According to the data, she and Armas supposedly shared the same father. Her gut tightened. No way could this awful man be her biological father.

"Everything all right?" The special agent's brow wrinkled.

What would happen once the office read the report? Would she be at risk of becoming the 'experiment' Demarco had feared for himself? What about Chad? Too much came at her all at once.

She smiled. It didn't feel like a real smile, but she hoped

it passed muster with the two men. "I'm all right. Maybe a little hungry." She checked her watch. "We had breakfast so early this morning."

"When will I be allowed to call my office?" Allwood placed his body between her and Angel. "This is ridiculous. You can't hold me. The lieutenant will set you straight."

"Shut up." Angel shoved the older man aside. "Where's Orr?" he asked Charlie.

The commander, at that very moment, exited the lab with a small Styrofoam cooler. "Samples and tests acquired."

As Orr and Angel discussed the next steps in handling Allwood, Charlie's mind flitted somewhere else. How was it possible Harrison Cutter was not her real father? Had her mother lied to him—and to her and her brother—for the last twenty plus years? She itched to pick up the phone and call her parents. Confront them. It didn't make any sense. She needed to hear from both her mother and father the test results were wrong. Dr. Stern and the NSA had been mistaken. There was no other possible explanation. Unless Chad knew something she didn't—?

"Petty Officer Cutter, are you with us?" Orr snapped his fingers in front of her face. "It seems as if you drifted off there for a moment."

"Yes." Her face heated. "I was wondering if we shouldn't call Kellerman to pick us up, return us to Nellis." Most of her thoughts were focused on her next steps. She had to call Chad. He had a right to know the same information she'd been given. If he knew anything at all, maybe it would give her clarity and a path forward.

"That's what Demarco just said." Orr crossed his arms. "Are you okay? You look a little pale."

She needed time away to think, to process, to analyze. All of this was too much to handle, plus keep her mind on her work and deal with her confused feelings for Angel. Her ears began to ring, and her vision faded to a dark tunnel. "I'm not feeling so well." Her knees buckled under her.

Angel rushed to catch her. "I've got her, sir." His solid arms wrapped around her. "She said she felt hungry earlier. Maybe she didn't have enough to eat this morning. I'll walk her to the cafeteria."

"Ever the gallant hero," scoffed Allwood with a roll of his eyes.

Angel's secure hold comforted her. If only she could confide in him, trust him. But he hated Allwood, and if he got wind of the DNA results his hatred would surely extend to her. "Yes, something to eat," she mumbled.

"Sir," Angel said, "if you can escort Allwood outside, we'll join you as soon as we can."

Charlie found her footing, and Angel curved an arm around her waist. "Lean on me. You'll be all right. I'm sorry. I didn't realize you were feeling that badly."

The commander eyed Charlie's physical state. "We'll wait out in the parking lot in the SUV." Orr hefted the cooler and jerked his chin in the direction of the exit. "Get moving, Allwood."

"Kellerman will know what to do." The professor sneered. "This is completely ridiculous. I didn't kill anyone."

"We'll see what the evidence says," Orr said. The two men walked together down the hall, the commander's free hand tightly gripped the professor's upper arm.

Angel leaned into Charlie's hair and kissed the top of her head. "Let's get you something to eat."

Shivers ran down her arms at the gentle kiss. She didn't want to be attracted to him anymore, but her body betrayed her. Damn him for being so chivalrous. "I'm sure I only need something to drink, and I'll be fine." She pushed out of his grip.

His posture stiffened. "Right. The cafeteria's this way." He led her in the opposite direction of Orr and Allwood.

She didn't care anymore if she hurt his feelings. Her whole life had blown up with one phone call. If those results put her in danger, then they put her brother in danger, too. And heaven forbid anyone touched him. Not on her watch.

CHAPTER 8

"WHERE'S KELLERMAN?" Commander Orr asked the chief when he arrived behind the wheel of the Ford Excursion. "Don't tell me you left him behind because he annoyed you." A believable possibility considering how many times Ricard had complained to him about Kellerman's obnoxious know-it-all attitude.

"He disappeared." Ricard shrugged. "Who's this guy?" He made a face at the sight of Allwood.

"Never mind about him. What do you mean Kellerman disappeared?" Orr gripped Allwood's arm more tightly. "What do you know about this?"

"Nothing. How could I? You've had me tied up for hours." Allwood lifted his plasticuffed wrists and grimaced. "When am I allowed a phone call? The base commander will be angry. We have a visiting senator who expected me this evening for a dinner engagement. The funding she could secure for my project—"

"Shut up." The man was a blowhard. How could the LT

stand this guy? "Where is Kellerman?" he asked the chief for a second time.

"The sample collection was a bust, by the way, the city was finishing the clean up as we arrived. Green shit every-where. Wouldn't let us within ten feet of any of it." The chief heavily stepped out of the SUV, which he'd parked along the curb clearly marked: *Emergency Use Only.* "Anyway, a few minutes later he got a phone call. Didn't want me to hear it. Wandered back up toward the road. And that's the last I saw of him. Thank God I had the spare key."

"What the hell?" Orr knew he never should've trusted the little prick. Always so smug about everything. Even the first day on the job. "Can you track his cell?"

"I'm the equipment guy; the LT was the tech expert." Ricard leaned against the black SUV and then flinched. "Ouch, that's fucking hot. Stupid Arizona."

"So you've lost one of your men, commander." Allwood raised his chin and exposed his longer-than-normal neck. "That's too bad. Now what will we do?"

Orr yanked open the sliding side door. "You are going to sit in here, while the Chief and I talk. And if I find out you and Kellerman were up to something, the NCIS is going to come knocking on your door, senator or no senator." He grabbed the professor by the wrists and forced him into the vehicle. Before the man could protest, Orr slammed the door shut in his face.

"Where's Cutter and Demarco?" Ricard took a wide stance and set his hands on his hips.

"They'll be here shortly." Orr headed to the back of the Excursion, opened the door, set the cooler in the back, and hid Demarco's gun under the rear seat. He'd deal with that later. "I've got lab evidence in there that's going to prove our survivor was murdered."

"What?" Ricard swung his head from Orr to the SUV and back, putting two and two together. "That jerk do it?"

"A high likelihood, yes." How was he going to convince a senator, a base commander, and probably a bunch of other muckety-mucks at Area 51 that their precious professor was a murderer? "He's coming back to DC with us until I can prove it."

"Shit, sir." Ricard rubbed a hand over his short, military-style haircut. "What do we do about Kellerman?"

"Until we can prove otherwise, I consider him an accomplice, and quite possibly the mastermind of this whole thing."

"Kellerman? That dweeb?" Ricard scoffed.

"He managed to fool us for months. Who knows how much information he's been sharing with Allwood." Orr thought through recent events and when their team might have been betrayed. "I'll bet he shared samples from his North Dakota trip with his pal. Who knows what else."

"So what's this Allwood been up to?"

"I don't know, but I'm sure going to find out."

Demarco and Cutter exited from the hospital.

"We've got six hours before our flight back home," Orr said. "I want the body, the samples, and Allwood loaded and ready to fly before nineteen-hundred. I'll take Demarco and make a plan regarding Kellerman. He might have some ideas about what tools are available to help."

"How will you get back to Nellis?" Chief asked.

"Don't worry. We'll figure something out." The commander turned his attention toward Demarco. "Special Agent, I've got a job for you."

CHAPTER 9

SWEAT RAN down Kellerman's face. Jogging a few blocks from the crash site had him dripping with the stuff. All those hours spent keeping in shape for the bi-annual Navy physical fitness test couldn't overcome the relentless heat of Arizona in late summer. He wiped his brow with the back of his hand and headed into the confusion of streets opposite the bridge.

Chief would notice he'd disappeared any minute. He didn't have much time to work a plan. The distraction of the city employees hosing down the crash area had been the perfect opportunity to slip away.

Allwood had called him well over an hour ago. The necessary task had been done. Although it made Kellerman's stomach roll at the thought, Allwood's explanation made sense: any survivors posed a risk to the professor and his ultimate goal. And Kellerman would do anything to protect that goal. He'd been promised a place at the professor's side. His right-hand man as they traveled through time together, exploring, learning, and dominating the past with advanced knowledge no ancient human could understand. Kellerman's tech expertise combined with the professor's knowledge of the pods and their capabilities would make them a powerful duo.

He stepped into the street.

A horn honked.

"Hey, watch where you're going." A middle aged woman in a compact SUV rolled down her window to scold him. "Do you want to get killed?"

He held up his hand and cleared out of the road. "Sorry."

But could he help it if his mind wandered? He and the professor were on the cusp of completing the formula and building pods that worked. Really worked. After all this time. Incredible.

With the heat beating down, Kellerman slowed to a walk. He checked over his shoulder. Nobody had followed him. He'd managed to slip away without being caught.

He looked at his phone for a text from Allwood. The professor had promised to pick him up after the stop at the hospital and transport him back to the Groom Lake warehouse. His time on the NCIS-A team was coming to a close. With his backdoor access to the office files in DC finally up and running, the professor would have everything he needed to finalize the formula. Charlie's notes on the manuscript, the doctor's data on the samples they'd retrieved—it all brought the professor closer and closer to solving the puzzle of the pods.

A new text appeared in his conversation with Allwood, but it was a garble of letters. Nonsense. What did it mean? Was everything under control?

He paused under the shade of a eucalyptus tree and

stared at his phone screen. He typed another message in the encrypted app they used:

Ready for pickup.

As he waited for a response, he noticed he'd received a new email in his secondary account. The one that forwarded any new files placed in the office system.

The subject line of the email read: *DNA Results*. It had come from the NSA lab to which Dr. Stern had sent the samples.

He clicked on the email and opened it.

As he read the results of the DNA comparisons, his stomach hardened.

It couldn't be. Not that bitch. Impossible.

Allwood had never said a thing.

A daughter? Charlie Fucking Cutter was his daughter?

The realization that the boy was Allwood's had been shock enough. An unforeseen wrinkle in his plan to serve by the professor's side. But a boy so young? Allwood wouldn't be interested in exploring time with a toddler. Even though he'd assigned Kellerman the task of retrieving the kid before he'd fallen ill...he didn't seriously think Allwood would bring him along? Would he?

But Charlie?

Pain radiated from his jaw. He had clenched his teeth —hard.

She'd translated the Voynich manuscript.

Allwood had been impressed with the young woman's capabilities and had been overjoyed when Kellerman reported she'd begun to tackle the formula page with the missing text.

After sacrificing everything for Allwood—his relationship with his brother, his oath to adhere to the restrictions of a Top Secret clearance, his career in the Navy—would the professor reward him? Or would Allwood shunt him aside for a newly discovered daughter with incredible capabilities?

Since he was the only one in the office who knew the truth and the only one who had access to the DNA file besides Dr. Stern, perhaps he should keep this information to himself. Why share it? Why jeopardize his place next to Allwood?

With no response to his text, Kellerman mulled over his next steps. Could Allwood have been discovered? Thank God he'd installed a tracking app months ago to make sure the professor stayed true to his promises. Watching his mentor's whereabouts had given him a modicum of peace. And now the app might save the professor's ass if something had gone awry with the plan.

He tapped on it.

Shit.

Allwood's yellow dot glowed brightly on the map—he was outside the hospital in the parking lot. However, the yellow dots of Commander Orr, Charlie, and Chief Ricard were clustered around him. The only person on the team he couldn't track was Demarco with his low tech flip phone. But if those three were together, he'd bet dollars to donuts Demarco was with them.

Kellerman stroked an eyebrow. The cluster of dots could only mean one thing: Allwood was in trouble.

CHAPTER 10

WHEN THE COMMANDER mentioned he had a job for him, Demarco hesitated. After years of searching for the bastard, he didn't want to let Allwood out of his sight. "What do you need, sir?"

Charlie opened the sliding door to expose the professor seated behind the driver's seat. Instantly, Demarco's anger flared up.

"Kellerman's gone missing, I think our fears he may be leaking information to your friend here have been realized." Orr nodded in Allwood's direction.

The 'professor'—what a joke he'd given himself that moniker—expelled air through his nose. "I had nothing to do with it. My project has the full backing of the United States Government and has for twenty years. The lieutenant was merely another officer in my lab. I barely knew him."

"That's not how he described it to us before we arrived," Orr said.

"The lieutenant is an arrogant man." Allwood raised his eyebrows and gave a glassy stare. "Why do you think I fired him from my office and was glad to see him receive a new assignment?"

"Shut up, already." Demarco stepped menacingly toward the restrained man sitting calmly in the air conditioning. One more word, and he'd feel the need to pummel him again.

"Did you already search him?" The chief, although quite a few inches shorter than the reedy Allwood, outweighed him by fifty pounds easy. He scanned the professor up and down.

Shit. How did he forget to search his pockets? "Things happened kind of quickly."

"He attacked me like a wild animal," Allwood said as Ricard helped him out of the vehicle to pat him down. "I might have to sue."

"A wallet." Ricard tossed it onto the sidewalk.

The commander picked it up.

"A syringe and a cell phone." The chief locked eyes with Orr as he held the capped syringe in his hand. "Sir?"

"Let's put that in the cooler with the lab samples." Carefully, Orr plucked the syringe from Ricard's hand and carried it to the back of the SUV. "Quite possibly he injected the survivor with whatever's in this thing. Dr. Stern is about to have her hands full."

Demarco grabbed the cell phone and turned it over in his hands.

Could be a lot of secrets on this thing. Including what Allwood had been up to all these years. Back in the ER Allwood had accused him of damaging Risa's pod, which sent her too far back in time. Could similar damage he'd inflicted on Allwood's pod have caused him to land far earlier than he intended?

"Charlie, can you unlock this?" He'd adapted relatively well to all the bizarre technology around him, but when stressed, he had trouble being patient. And figuring out how to unlock a cell phone when he wanted to throttle the man being re-loaded into the SUV counted as one of those times.

Charlie took the phone from him. "Sure," she said quietly.

Something was up with her since the minute they'd met up in the hall outside the lab. Was the death of the time traveling woman too much for her? Maybe she was more sensitive than he realized.

He swept her figure. Where did the confident, intelligent woman go? Her posture slumped, and her gaze was fixed on their captive.

"Hold on, Chief," she said. "Could you face me, please?" Her voice was a squeak as she addressed the man in plasticuffs.

Allwood continued climbing into the vehicle as if he hadn't heard her.

"Hey, professor, the lady needs your face." Chief Ricard forced Allwood's head to turn by grabbing his chin.

"Thanks." She held up the phone screen to the man's face, and the facial recognition kicked into gear. "We're in."

Chief loaded Allwood into the SUV for a second time and slammed the door.

"Demarco, we need to track down Kellerman now." Commander Orr redirected focus. "He doesn't have a vehicle, and we know he ran off from the crash site. What should our next steps be?"

"Maybe he called an Uber?" Charlie said as she scrolled through emails and texts. "Most of this is routine communications. I don't see anything here that connects to Kellerman."

"What about encrypted apps?" Orr asked.

A light came on in Charlie's eyes, and she tapped and scrolled on the phone screen.

Demarco looked at his watch. "It's been fifteen or twenty minutes since the LT probably fled the scene. In this heat, he could maybe make it a half-mile." The sun was like a ball of fire. Even in good shape, the temperature would impact a man's stamina.

"Since the crash occurred on the banks of the Lake, we only have one direction he could've run." Orr and Demarco locked eyes. "Let's do a sweep."

Demarco nodded. Lake Havasu was one third retirees, so a young, fit man in his late twenties should stand out on the streets.

"So I'm coming with you?" Charlie asked with a hopeful uptilt to her voice. She stood on the sidewalk making no move to join the chief.

"Ricard needs someone to keep an eye on the prisoner while he drives. Head straight to the base. Chief can secure him in the plane. We'll meet you there." Orr checked his watch. "Kellerman's the priority. He's our leaker and every minute he's out there, our team and our work is in jeopardy of being exposed."

"Right. I'll see you at Nellis." She frowned and then climbed into the passenger seat.

Why was Charlie so reluctant to go with Ricard?

CHAPTER 11

CHIEF RICARD PULLED AWAY from the curb. "I hope they find that piece of shit. They should put Kellerman away for twenty years. Leaking classified materials. I knew he couldn't be trusted. The minute he walked into the office— all pressed and perfect with that stick up his ass."

Charlie nodded, but her mind was elsewhere. The man seated behind her was her birth father. Dr. Stern had told her, so it must be true. The NSA lab likely had some of the best equipment and best scientists in the field. How was she supposed to reconcile this new information and fit it into her life history? Who was Harrison Cutter? Why did her mother lie to her?

She half-turned her body. "We know you arrived in one of the pods, professor."

Ricard flinched and pressed a bit too hard on the gas, causing the SUV to lurch forward onto the street. "What the fuck?"

Charlie ignored him. Who cared what she divulged now? The minute they all returned to the office, everyone would know her DNA tied her to Armas. Everyone would be looking at her. Might as well put all her cards on the table. She wanted to know the truth.

"You mentioned your work goes back twenty years." Her gut twisted. She thought back to the radar data presented to them upon landing in Nellis. "So when did you arrive? 1996? In Texas?" Her brightly colored memories of her childhood on the Naval Base in Corpus Christi turned faded and gray. Something had happened there. Something before she was born that her mother had kept from her.

"Goddammit, Cutter, what in the hell is going on?" Ricard swung them onto the highway to head back to the Air Force base.

Allwood raised an eyebrow. "So Demarco told you everything?"

"If you two don't tell me what the fuck is happening here, I swear—" Ricard's face turned bright red.

"Our professor is a time traveler," she explained to the chief. "He's been here for years. Demarco figured it out." That was as much as she wanted to say. Maybe Ricard would puzzle the rest out eventually, but for now it was all about learning the truth of her parentage.

"If you have the data, you already know that's when I arrived." Allwood leaned back in his seat. "Why do these questions matter?"

"You mean this shit is real?" Ricard's shoulders relaxed, and his chin dipped. His tough guy demeanor melted away in seconds once he realized the truth: time travel was real. The last one on their team to believe it.

"I want to know what you did when you climbed out of that pod." Her thumb absentmindedly rubbed across the screen of his phone. What was he hiding in the encrypted chat app she'd found? "How did you manage to survive? How did you end up as a respected researcher at Area 51?"

Allwood lifted a shoulder. "I made friends. I'm sure Demarco told you a similar story. You'd be surprised how easy it is to find people sympathetic and willing to help a man in need."

"Friends?" Before her mother met Harrison, what had her story been? Charlie had so few details to build on. The information had been sparse: maybe a job on base or was it a friend on base? If she only had some privacy and a few minutes to call her mother or Chad, maybe she would be able to uncover the truth.

"Why would Demarco have a similar story?" Ricard, although focused on the road ahead, managed to pick up on the slightest of hints.

Allwood's eyes lit up. "Ah, so not everyone knows the truth. I see. Demarco always was a miscreant. Stirring up trouble for no reason. He wouldn't leave me alone. He has some kind of vendetta against me."

"Cutter, you'd better tell me the goddamn truth." Chief's hands gripped the steering wheel so tight his fingers turned white "Who the fuck is Demarco?"

"That's not important right now." Charlie felt the conversation slipping away from her. She'd wanted answers about Allwood, about her, about her family history. These answers couldn't wait. She needed them now. Needed to know if her brother would be in danger.

"Petty Officer Cutter." Chief's sharp tone reminded her that he was still her superior. He outranked her by several steps. "I am demanding you tell me what is going on here. Why is this guy talking about Demarco?"

"Oh my, didn't she tell you?" Allwood chuckled. "Angel Demarco followed me here in one of my machines. He fooled you into believing he's something he's not. That badge you let him carry around? And the lies he probably told to convince you of his background? He's a farmer's son. He barely knows how to tie his own shoes."

Charlie froze. She stared out the window in a daze.

"And he's alone with Commander Orr? Who the fuck is he?" Ricard swerved the SUV across all lanes of traffic to the shoulder. A car behind them honked at the dangerous move. He braked hard, and they jerked to a dead stop on the side of the highway. "Cutter, what did you do?

CHAPTER 12

DEMARCO JOGGED another block over from the hospital. He and Orr had split up to cover more ground. They had to find Kellerman before he slipped away—and maybe it already was too late. That bastard.

Although a breeze kicked up, the sweat dripped from his forehead. It reminded him of haying season back home. Hot, dirty work. But they'd had to keep working until the job was done. Spoiled hay wouldn't feed the horses and cows through the winter.

He couldn't stop until this job was done either. Kellerman had been sharing NCIS-A secrets with Allwood. Maybe even keeping information from them to make their jobs harder. The break-in at the motel in North Dakota had probably been his doing and who knows what he'd shared since then. Translations? Reports? What about the arrival of Armas?

An odd sensation filled his chest when he thought of the boy. But he brushed it off.

He rounded a corner and scanned the street.

The sight of a dark haired man at the end of the block caught his eye.

Could that be Kellerman?

He slowed his jog to a walk so as not to draw attention to himself.

The man had his back to him allowing Demarco the opportunity to close in without fear of being seen. As he drew nearer, his breathing slowed. His target turned so that his profile was visible, and he looked down at his phone.

No mistaking. It was Kellerman.

Demarco paused behind a parked delivery van that provided him some cover, pulled out his phone, and called Orr.

"I've got him. We're on Willow Avenue." He kept his gaze fixated on the lieutenant. "About five blocks down from Emerald Drive."

"I'm on my way. Detain him until I get there."

"Yes, sir." He hung up.

Kellerman turned and looked up the street. Their eyes met.

Shit.

The lieutenant bolted.

Demarco chased after at full speed. His shorter stature and solid body mass slowed him down, compared to the taller, leaner Kellerman.

A gray-haired man walking a dachshund blocked his route. Demarco pushed off the man's shoulder, spun, and barely avoided tangling his legs in the leash.

"Hey!" the surprised dog walker yelled.

But he had no time for apologies. Kellerman had crossed the street and was headed between two houses.

Demarco dug as deep as he could to draw on the last bit of energy he had. His thigh muscles burned. If he'd been fresh off the farm, he would've been able to best the younger man, but years of less physical living had reduced his stamina.

"Fuck!" He rounded the corner of the southwestern style home. Gravel kicked up under his heels.

A motorcycle flew past, practically knocking him to the ground.

Kellerman.

Instinctually, he changed direction to chase after him, but Kellerman sped away toward the highway and disappeared in seconds.

Demarco slowed to a halt and leaned over, resting his hands on his knees to catch his breath. He'd failed. He'd lost him.

"Dammit." They'd never catch him now. Kellerman would be stupid to show his face at their offices or anywhere near the Washington Navy Yard. Even Area 51 should be off limits once they received the news. The whole of the military would be on high alert for Lieutenant Cole Kellerman.

A RAV4 pulled up next to him with a blonde woman in her late forties in the driver's seat. The back passenger window rolled down. Commander Orr's sweaty face appeared. "Get in. We can catch him."

Without saying a word, Demarco skipped around the back of the Toyota and climbed in.

CHAPTER 13

RICARD PICKED up his cell phone from the center console and dialed a number. "I can't believe you left the commander with some impostor." Chief's eyes bulged.

"Demarco's not an impostor." Charlie looked down at her hands in her lap. What did it matter what chief thought of Demarco, of her, of this whole big mess blowing up in their faces? Her whole sense of self had been ripped out from under her. Her mother was a liar, her father wasn't even her father, and her brother? What would he think when he heard the news? He idolized Harrison Cutter. He'd modeled his whole life after their father—correction—stepfather. It would devastate him.

Allwood clucked his tongue. "What a terrible shame your little investigation is falling apart. Your office will be disbanded by morning once I bend the senator's ear. I should've shut you down months ago. I could have you know."

Charlie's heart beat sluggishly. The work she'd abandoned and then rediscovered had brought her so much satisfaction—the Voynich manuscript—now she wished she'd never come across it. If she could only wish herself away from this spot on the side of the highway and instead land in Navy survival school in Maine to pursue her original dream. What would happen to her now? Would she be kicked out of the military for her connection to Allwood? Would she lose her clearance? What implications did this have for her future? In less than twenty-four hours news of her parentage would be revealed to the team. What was her plan?

"Commander, are you with Demarco?" Chief asked. His thumb beat out a nervous rhythm on the steering wheel. He was silent for a few seconds. "What? Where is that little SOB?" Without a word of explanation to Charlie, Chief hopped out of the vehicle.

"Chief?" She leaned forward to catch a glimpse of where he went. What had Orr told him?

"So, Cutter is it?" Allwood's voice sounded as smooth as fresh ice.

Chief stood on the asphalt and scanned the lanes of traffic. Although she was curious what the commander may have told Ricard, this might be her only opportunity alone with Allwood. Should she ask him more questions that might divulge their connection?

She blinked a few times. "Petty Officer Cutter, yes."

"I hear you haven't been with the office very long."

"Kellerman tell you that?"

Allwood didn't answer. "If you still want to have a career when this is all over, you might want to consider your actions going forward."

"Is that a threat?" Her gaze became unfocused.

"I happen to know people in very high places who could be valuable to you."

"I don't need your help." A high pitched buzzing sounded in her ears.

The professor expelled air out his nose. "Everyone needs someone's help. Do you think Demarco was smart enough to get where he is on his own? Even he had to rely on someone."

She tumbled that over in her brain. She didn't want to listen to what Allwood had to say about Angel. She'd heard the story from his side and trusted him far more than a man who would abandon the mother of his children. What kind of heartless, selfish person would do that?

Chief yanked open the door. "Buckle up, we're on a mission." Before Charlie could check her seatbelt, Ricard pressed on the gas and exploded forward to rejoin the traffic on the highway.

She grabbed the handle on the door to keep from bouncing out of her seat. "What's going on?"

"That little bastard Kellerman stole a motorcycle, and we're gonna catch his ass." Ricard hunched over his steering wheel and checked his mirrors before swerving into the far left lane. "See that yellow and black Suzuki up there?"

She tilted her head until she saw the motorcycle several cars ahead of them and then nodded.

"Kellerman's on the run, and we're going to be the ones to stop him."

"What about taking the prisoner to Nellis and catching our flight home?"

Ricard gunned it, made a quick right into the middle lane, and then cut off a red Honda Civic in the fast lane. "I don't give a flying fuck about missing the goddamn plane,

Cutter. This jackass is a criminal, and we need to shut him down. We'll figure out the rest later."

Allwood's silence in the back was notable.

Charlie turned to face him. "Where would he be going, professor?" She pushed out of her mind the fact the man with the maniacal grin on his face and a strange gleam in his eye was her biological father.

The SUV bumped over a pothole. She grabbed the head-rest to steady herself, but still managed to bite her tongue.

The professor shrugged. His earlier loquaciousness disappeared.

But it didn't take a genius to figure out Kellerman's desti-nation. "He's headed to the one place he knows, the one place he feels safe."

She and Ricard exchanged glances.

"Area 51," they said simultaneously.

CHAPTER 14

KELLERMAN PUSHED the motorcycle to its limits. Knowing the capabilities of Demarco, he'd find a way to catch up to him. He'd steal a car, hijack a bus—something. He'd learned in the last few months never to underestimate the special agent. As he zipped through traffic, weaving in and out of lanes to put as much distance between him and Lake Havasu as he could, he began to make a mental plan.

Groom Lake was his only option. He could hide there. And, if he was lucky, he could disappear from there, too.

The professor might be ticked, as it deviated from their plan, but he didn't care. The minute he'd seen the news come across his phone about Charlie, he knew he didn't have much time. The way the professor had talked about his long-lost wife, he knew loyalty to family and to his blood would surpass any loyalty he held toward Kellerman. No matter how much he'd sacrificed for the man. Charlie had changed everything. Damn her.

The heat of the midday Arizona sun beat down on his back. He had hours to ride before he'd reach his destination.

The base was ninety minutes beyond Nellis. Checking his gas gauge, he mentally calculated if he had enough.

Maybe.

If he were lucky.

———

Demarco sat next to the commander in the back of the hired SUV. "We've got to catch up to him, sir."

"Ricard can handle it."

Their driver, Pam, drove the speed limit down the highway. Demarco wanted to leap into the front, shove her out of the seat, and take over. Kellerman had to be stopped, and he had to ensure Allwood was secured. Too many loose ends. His mind ran into two directions at once. Then there was Charlie. Trapped with a madman. Ricard had no idea of the capabilities Allwood had to deceive, to charm, to draw a victim into his way of thinking.

He'd managed to dupe hundreds of people to give over their lives to him, their very bodies to his experiments. Would he manage to convince Ricard to do his bidding? To let him go? Or something worse?

His stomach churned.

Which was the correct action to take?

"You said to head toward Vegas," Pam said in a bright voice. "I need to be home by supper time. Chester's expecting me. He won't like it if I don't have his food waiting for him when he comes home. Are you going to the airport? A hotel?"

"Take us to Nellis." The commander made his choice. They were going to play the supporting role.

Demarco itched to take control. He was so close to taking

down Allwood. So close. And now they were going to sit on their hands at Nellis and do nothing?

"What are we going to do there, sir? You expect Cutter and Ricard to handle the professor *and* chase down Kellerman?"

"You two military?" Pam switched from the middle lane to the slower right lane, as if she were enjoying the ride and didn't want it to end any sooner than it had to. "My Chester's a former Marine. Did two tours somewhere. Maybe Iraq? He doesn't like to talk about it."

Both men ignored Pam's inquiry. "We don't have any choice," said Orr.

"Of course we have a choice." Demarco's mind darkened. Orr was too much of a regulations man. A rules follower. That sort of thinking would destroy any chance he had of attaining his goal. Allwood was within his grasp. If any time was the right time to risk the security of his position, it was now. "Pam, pull over."

"What?" In the rearview mirror, Pam's gaze locked with his.

"I don't want to have to ask again, please." He lowered his voice a few notches. His dangerous voice. The voice he used when he'd killed some of Allwood's men in a time when guns didn't exist. When killing involved sweat and blood and looking into a man's eyes when you sliced his throat. "Pull over."

Commander Orr leaned forward, alarm in his eyes.

Demarco quickly captured the older man in a headlock, his arm tight across Orr's throat. "Don't, sir."

"I don't understand. This is an Uber." Pam's voice trembled and ratcheted up to a higher pitch. "Just tell me where you want to go, and I'll take you there. You said Vegas: where in Vegas?"

The desperation he heard in her words cut him up inside. He wasn't the bad guy here, but she wouldn't understand. The commander wouldn't understand.

Demarco's arm tightened on Orr's windpipe. The man struggled under the unexpected pressure. His eyes bugged out. Disbelief was etched into his features as his trusted security officer choked him into unconsciousness. He clawed at Demarco's solid arm, the elbow bent just enough to prevent the flow of oxygen to his brain.

"I'm sorry, sir." The special agent felt his superior go limp in his arms.

Pam screamed.

Demarco asked one more time, "Pull over, Pam."

Pam turned on her signal and took the off-ramp—a deserted road miles from anywhere. Her whole body shook. "P-please. I don't have any money."

As the car stopped near the overpass, Demarco opened the back door and used his feet to shove Orr out onto the shoulder. "I don't want your money. I want your car."

The blonde woman nodded, tears rolling down her cheeks. "Yes, take it. Whatever you want." She leapt from the vehicle and ran toward the traffic at the other end of the off-ramp.

Demarco stepped over the unconscious body of his boss, climbed into the driver's seat, and sped back onto the highway.

———

Several drivers flipped off Ricard. He'd cut them off making hazardous lane switches and passing slower cars on the right. Every time the SUV came within a few car lengths of Kellerman, the lieutenant managed to zip between cars or even two semi-trucks.

"Shit," Ricard swore under his breath. "When did Kellerman learn to drive a bike like that?"

Allwood sat silently in the back. Charlie relished it. For now, she wanted to focus on making sure Ricard didn't kill them. She didn't need to be distracted by thoughts about her mother, her brother, and her birth father. That would have to wait until later.

"We're hours away from Area 51," she pointed out. "We've got plenty of time to catch him. Maybe he'll run out of gas."

Ricard took a quick glance at the gas gauge. "Dammit."

Charlie covered her mouth with her hand. "Oh, no."

"Oh, fucking, yes. This behemoth gets fifteen miles to the gallon, and we're at a quarter tank." Ricard smacked his hand on the dashboard. "No way in hell we're letting that weasel get away."

She furrowed her brow. "Call the commander."

"You do it."

Charlie nodded, set Allwood's phone on the center console, and dug her own cell out of her purse.

Ricard looked down at the gauge for a second time. "Tell him we've got maybe fifty or sixty more miles and then we're out."

The phone rang and rang. "He's not picking up." She rubbed her free hand on her pant leg. The phone rang two more times. She showed him her phone screen. "He's not answering. Now what?"

"Fuck." Ricard dodged a Toyota Camry that had changed lanes right in front of him. "Gimme that." He snatched her phone away.

The SUV crossed over into another lane. A car honked.

"Keep your eyes on the road." Her adrenaline spiked.

"I got his stupid voicemail." Ricard tossed Charlie's phone at her. It clattered to the floor and landed under her seat.

"Hey. Be careful." She felt around underneath her for the smooth screen of her phone. "Should I try calling Demarco?"

"Yeah." Ricard wiped a sheen of sweat off his brow. "Demarco. They're together. Good thinking, Cutter."

Charlie came into contact with her phone. "Got it." She pressed Demarco's number.

"I see him!" Ricard's eyes lit up. "The fucker. Thought he could get away from me. I don't think so." He hunched over the steering wheel. "Let's see how fast this baby can go."

The SUV's eight-cylinder engine struggled to give Chief the additional power and speed he wanted.

"Not very," Allwood quipped from the back.

"Shut up." Ricard zoomed forward.

The phone rang several times. No answer. Charlie's gut twisted. Not good. Why weren't Orr or Demarco answering?

"Charlie?"

Hearing the familiar voice of the special agent alleviated some of the tension inside her.

"Angel," she breathed.

"You got him?" Ricard asked. "I see Kellerman's pansy-ass. Right up there. Stuck behind a Walmart truck and boxed in by the Ford F-150."

"Yes, he picked up." She glanced at the cars in front of them. Distantly, almost two hundred yards away, she could barely make out the bright yellow motorcycle behind the semi.

"I've got something to do Charlie." Angel's voice had an odd quality to it.

"What are you talking about?"

"Where are you?" he asked.

"We're following Kellerman. That's why I called."

"What road marker are you near?"

"What? I don't know." She felt a tingling in her chest. "Look, Demarco, we tried calling Orr, he didn't pick up. We aren't going to be able to follow Kellerman much longer. We're going to run out of gas. We think he's headed for Area 51. Can you and the Commander catch up to us?"

"Orr's not available right now."

"Okay." What a strange way of wording it. What did he mean by that? "Can you catch up to us?" They passed a green directional sign. "We're right near Exit 141 just past Needles."

"141. Thank you, Charlie."

The line went dead.

CHAPTER 15

DEMARCO ZOOMED THROUGH TRAFFIC. Although he'd landed in a time period with vehicles capable of incredibly high speeds, he'd never driven so quickly. The desert landscape flashed past. He kept his gaze focused on the mile markers, barely comprehending them as he flew past.

A green directional sign above the highway announced Exit 141 to Needles in two miles.

Driving at—he glanced at the speedometer—over one-hundred miles an hour should mean he'd catch up to his team in less than two minutes.

As he thought about what he had to do, a black emptiness filled him.

Charlie was in that car. So was Ricard.

But he had no choice.

Orr and the others on the team weren't taking this seriously. They thought they could arrest Allwood, put him in jail, send him through the ridiculously slow and tainted court system, and end up with a guilty verdict. But he knew better. He knew Allwood would never stop. The minute he was a free man, he'd start up right where he left off. The man was obsessed with perfection. He'd never let go of his twisted vision for the human race: to manipulate and alter them to the point that no one would recognize themselves as human anymore. And Demarco had to stop him.

He swerved around a silver two-door car and spied a large, black SUV in the distance that sped past other vehicles around it. That had to be Ricard.

As the cars passed by the exit for Needles, the traffic thinned and the lanes narrowed down to two.

Just what he needed to pull off a move.

Charlie, I'm sorry.

He approached the team's vehicle from behind. He'd seen a PIT maneuver completed successfully multiple times in online videos. Although he'd intended to learn all he could about law enforcement early in his arrival in order to blend in and play the role he'd chosen as best suited to find Allwood, he never thought he'd actually have to use the maneuver himself.

Done correctly, the target vehicle should safely spin out into the shoulder.

He tightened his hands around the steering wheel and exhaled through his mouth.

It was time.

Demarco pressed on the gas lightly and drove partially onto the shoulder to approach Ricard from the correct side. Before the other vehicle had time to detect his presence, he aligned the front of his car with the rear tires and steered into them.

Shit.

He used more force than he'd intended.

The other vehicle lost traction and began to skid. The SUV turned in front of him.

For a split second, he caught sight of a terrified Charlie in the passenger's seat. He averted his gaze, because he couldn't watch what was about to happen.

He'd hit the vehicle too hard, and instead of slowing to a crooked stop in the shoulder, it tilted up and began to roll down an embankment.

A pain hit the back of his throat.

What had he done?

Envisioning an unconscious and injured Charlie, he slammed on the brakes, left his car running, and raced down the slope toward them. Someone on the highway surely saw what had happened and would be dialing 911 within seconds.

Ricard and Charlie would be fine.

He repeated that over and over in his head as he approached them.

Securing Allwood before the cops showed up was more important.

The SUV lay on its side.

He saw no movement, no attempt from anyone to climb out.

The blazing heat of the desert sun beat down on everything. If the engine caught fire, there could be a serious problem with dried grass and scrub brush everywhere.

"Help me," a faint voice called.

Demarco ran around the back end. Allwood lay twenty feet away from the crash site. He'd been thrown free of the vehicle at some point. Debris littered the ground. Without thinking, he picked up papers and a cardboard box full of vials that must've been in the back of the SUV as he made his way to the injured man.

Where was Charlie? Still inside?

Fuck.

He didn't have time to worry about her. This is why he'd remained alone for seven years. This is why he chose not to make friends or get close to anyone. For this very reason.

Why did he have to fall for her?

He dropped the box and the papers. "Get up."

"I can't," Allwood whined.

The man had a cut on his leg that bled freely and one of his arms looked mangled. Somehow he'd been freed from the plasticuffs in the wreck.

Demarco grabbed his uninjured arm. "Get the fuck up."

Allwood cried out in pain as the special agent forced him to stand. "I can't walk."

"Yes, you can." He twisted the older man's arm behind his back and pushed him toward the highway. "You're coming with me, and you're going to show me everything. Got it?"

"Angel?" Charlie was extricating herself out of the blown out passenger's side window. "What happened?"

Blood ran freely from a head wound, but otherwise Charlie appeared uninjured.

Demarco's chest tightened. "There was an accident." He relaxed his grip on Allwood. "Don't make a move, bastard, or I'll break this arm, too," he spat out.

"Did we hit something?" She sat on the edge of the door and surveyed the ground below.

"Yes," he lied. "I think you blew a tire and swerved off the highway. I have to secure Allwood. Then, I'll come back and help."

Charlie nodded weakly. "Okay. Right." She looked down into the vehicle. "Ricard looks bad, Angel."

"He'll be okay, Charlie. The police will be here any minute." As he said the words, he could hear the faint sound of sirens in the distance. "Stay there. I'll be right back."

But he knew he wouldn't be back, and he hated himself for it.

What would she think when he drove off? That he'd used her? That everything he'd said to her was lies? Probably.

"My head really hurts." She touched a hand to her wound and then looked at the blood on her fingers.

"I know. You'll be okay." He had to ignore the voice inside that told him to stay, to make sure she was okay, to check on Ricard. "Come on, Allwood."

"Where's the commander?" she asked.

His mind flicked to when he'd pushed an unconscious Orr out of the Uber and left the driver running away in fear.

Demarco's grip on Allwood became like iron. "I'll be right back." He couldn't look at her anymore.

He pushed the older man up the slope and to his car at the top. If the cops showed, they'd not only see the damage, but they'd probably run the plate, find out it was stolen, and arrest him. He only had a few minutes to escape.

Charlie would be fine.

Charlie would be just fine.

It would be better for her to hate him, anyway. What could he possibly give her? He was a mess. He wasn't built to handle more than one emotion at a time. And his whole reason for being after finding himself hundreds of years in the past had been to capture this man. This lunatic. This disgusting 'professor' who'd harmed dozens of innocent people. Love? He didn't have space for that in this bizarre life he'd found himself in. She was better off without him.

Opening up the passenger's side door, he flung Allwood inside. He could keep a better eye on him up front.

"You have to take me to the hospital," Allwood complained when Demarco climbed into the driver's seat.

A flush of heat flooded Demarco's body. He snapped his seatbelt, shifted the car into drive, and pressed on the gas. "Shut the hell up. You're going to take me to your lab, show me everything, and then we're going to burn it all down."

Demarco hoped to God he didn't strangle the man before he could achieve all of that. Because his fingers itched to do it. He'd never hated a man so much. A deep, black, ugly hate festered inside him and threatened to consume him.

Allwood sat silently next to him. His captive had realized there was no way out, and the only option was to obey.

In his rearview mirror, Demarco caught sight of red flashing lights. At least two police cars raced to the scene of the accident. Witnesses would probably be able to describe him, Allwood, and his vehicle. So he had to put as much distance between him and the wreck as he could.

Forgive me, Charlie.

A sign overhead read: Las Vegas – 108 miles.

He blasted his brain clear of worry and thoughts of Charlie and focused on his destination.

CHAPTER 16

INJURED AND CONFUSED, Charlie drew a deep breath through her nose at the sight of Angel at the bottom of the embankment. He'd recaptured Allwood and, despite her concerns about his loyalty to the team and his view of Genesis Project followers, was going to rescue her and Ricard. But then he'd dragged Allwood away, hopped in some car, and drove off in a cloud of dust. She couldn't believe it.

He'd abandoned them.

And where was Orr?

The bottom dropped out of her stomach.

Something wasn't right here.

Angel had Allwood in his hands and Kellerman in his sights. The worst possible person to be alone with either man. He had vengeance on his mind.

Before the authorities arrived, she hopped down into the overturned vehicle to check on Ricard's status. What else could she do? Everything she'd been working toward was about to be ripped away—her career, her family, her future.

Allwood was her father. As unbelievable as it sounded, according to Dr. Stern it was the truth. Within days, everyone would be looking at her and her brother. Would she and Chad be lumped into the same category as Allwood and his band of time travelers? Would they be questioned, studied, incarcerated? Her clearance would likely be revoked. His officer candidacy yanked. All because of their DNA.

Not only that, she'd likely be a target of Angel's rage. The very rage she saw on display only a few moments ago. Angel had been willing to abandon his girlfriend and his teammate for a chance at revenge. Would that feeling extend to her once he found out the truth?

Ricard groaned. The front end of the SUV had been crushed when the vehicle had flipped. The engine had been pushed inward, which pinned him under the steering wheel.

"Are you all right, Chief?"

He didn't answer.

She kicked away plastic and metal fragments that littered the interior to clear the view.

"Chief, are you hurt? Can you move?" She planted one foot on the side of the driver's seat and the other on the edge of the dashboard.

Was that her cell phone?

She grabbed it. The screen had a crack in it, but it appeared to be functional.

"Cutter? What happened?" Ricard's labored speech told her his breathing was compromised.

"We've been in an accident."

He struggled to break free of the steering wheel.

"The police are on their way. Try to relax."

She popped her head out the window to check for any approaching police cars. The sirens grew louder and louder. The only way Ricard would make it out of here was with help—serious help. But at least he was talking and alert.

Ricard lay still. "Where's Allwood?"

At least he remembered they had another passenger. "Don't worry about him."

"Where is he, Cutter?" Although his voice lacked its usual power, the demanding tone remained. "He's our responsibility. The commander is counting on us."

"I'll explain later." No point in telling him the truth at this stage. He was in shock. Any increase in his stress levels could be detrimental. "Let's focus on you. Breathe."

Hearing a door slam, she took another look outside. Two uniformed officers trotted down the embankment.

"Help is here." A sudden lightness filled her. "I'm going to let them know what happened and that we need some help getting you out of here."

Charlie pushed herself up and out of the window and sat on the edge.

"Miss," a female officer reached the wreck first. "Are you all right? An ambulance is on its way."

The other officer, tall and dark-haired, spoke into a radio attached to his shoulder.

"I think I'm okay, but my friend is pinned in the driver's seat."

"Phillips, we need fire and rescue," the officer said to her partner. "We've got another occupant trapped inside."

The male officer helped Charlie down to the ground. As the police went into rescue mode, she backed away.

What was the next step? How could she stop Angel?

She looked down at her damaged phone, unlocked it, selected a name from her contacts list, and pressed the call button.

CHAPTER 17

CHARLIE STOOD thirty feet away from the wreck, watching the fire crew bring down the Jaws of Life. As the phone rang on the other end, she bit the inside of her cheek. She'd really been hoping to have this conversation in person, but there was no time to waste.

"Charlie, hello!" Angela Cutter greeted her daughter in a bright voice. "Have you moved into your new place yet? I was thinking about some old curtains I have in the basement somewhere—"

"Mom, I need to ask you something important." Her insides quivered. "And I need you to be honest with me." She couldn't move on to the next step in her plan until she'd taken care of this.

"Honest?" Charlie imagined her mother twisting her wedding ring as she always did when nervous. "What are you talking about, sweetie?"

"My dad. I know."

A firefighter positioned the battery-operated jaws around one of the roof supports and switched on the power to cut through it. The noise made it difficult to hear. Charlie walked up toward the road to put some distance between her and the machine.

"What about your father? I don't understand."

Charlie swallowed. "Harrison Cutter isn't my father."

There was a long pause on the other end. Then, the sound of a door closing.

"Charlene, how dare you say such things." Her mother's voice became a harsh whisper. "Who told you these lies? Who?"

The panic in her mother's words came across loud and clear. Charlie had hit on the truth. Harrison Cutter wasn't her birth father. For some reason, having the fact confirmed made her chest ache.

"Byron Allwood is my real father." An EMT approached Charlie after noticing her injury. She waved him away. The cut on her head would have to wait.

Her mother gasped on the other end.

"You both were in Corpus Christi at the same time. Maybe you met on the base? But what I don't understand is why would you lie to me? To Chad? All these years. I don't understand."

"Chad can never know."

"Chad *will* know, Mom." She stared out at the traffic, wishing with all her might she was a normal person in a car headed home or to Las Vegas or to the airport. She wanted to be anywhere but here. "Why do you think I'm calling you? Why do you think I know? The truth is going to come out whether you like it or not. If you aren't going to explain it to Chad, I will."

"It will crush him, Charlie."

"I know." Charlie's gut twisted. Before she called her mom, she'd been angry, but now she felt only sadness. "But he'll find out whether you want him to or not. Wouldn't it be better to hear it from you?"

"Your father—we made a pact we'd never tell." Angela Cutter quietly cried. "How do I explain it to him?"

"There are DNA results. Indisputable. They found out at work—"

"At work?"

More emergency vehicles arrived, surrounding her on all sides. One police officer set out cones and blocked traffic from passing the scene in the right lane. "I can't tell you more than that, Mom."

"And Byron? He's still alive?"

"Yes."

"You've found him after all this time?" Her mother sounded shocked.

"Yes."

"I thought he was dead. All these years...and knowing I was carrying you two. Why would he do that?"

Her heart hurt for the young mother Angela Cutter had been more than twenty years ago. "I don't know."

"He abandoned me. Pregnant and unmarried. A job at the Px. I couldn't raise twins by myself."

"I'm sorry that happened to you." Tears pricked at her eyes. Her anger at being lied to gave way to sympathy for the loving, kind mother she'd known her whole life. Allwood had used her just like he'd used his followers. It had been all about himself, his needs, his desires, his dreams. Maybe Angel wasn't so wrong about his feelings toward Allwood.

"Your father—Harrison, I mean—he was so kind to me. A

customer who befriended me. Somehow it turned into—well, we got married. He promised he would raise you as his own."

"He did, Mom," Charlie said. "You did the right thing. He was a good father."

An EMT rolled a stretcher down the embankment. Maybe Ricard had been freed from the wreck.

"He still is, Charlie. If you'd only let him in."

A large, white pick-up truck emblazoned with a local tow truck service's logo drove down the embankment.

"Right now I'm more worried about Chad." Her scalp prickled. "I don't know how to get a hold of him. I tried texting him, and he's not answering."

"He's on a flight to Spain."

The EMT appeared on the shoulder with Ricard strapped to the gurney. The chief noticed her on the phone and weakly waved. Charlie faked a smile and waved back.

"I thought he was leaving in another couple of weeks?"

"He took some leave, so he could scout out a place to live. Housing is tight on base."

"Dammit." How was she going to protect her brother from five thousand miles away?

"I promise. I'll tell him."

The female police officer who'd been first on the scene approached her with a metal clipboard and a serious look on her face. "I have something I need to do, Mom. You have to make sure he knows. We have maybe a day, possibly less."

"I don't understand," her mother said.

"People might come looking for him. Bad people."

The officer raised her eyebrows.

"What are you saying—?"

Charlie turned away from the officer and whispered into

the phone. "Byron Allwood is not a good man. I don't know who he was when you met him, but he's not that man anymore. He's a fugitive. He murdered someone. And I have to make sure he's brought to justice."

"My God." Angela Cutter paused for a few seconds. "And Chad? Why would anyone be after Chad?"

"Because we are his children and that puts us at risk. There are people out there who think we are just as guilty because of our family connection." Charlie took a quick look over her shoulder. The officer wouldn't be patient for long.

"Guilty of what? How could either of you be guilty of a murder someone else committed? I don't understand."

"Please make sure you get a hold of Chad. Explain to him. Tell him he needs to be careful. Have him call me when he can. I need to talk to him."

"I'm sorry, sweetie. I'm sorry I didn't tell you the truth," her mother said.

"It's okay. I know you were only trying to protect us and give us the best life you could."

"And it was a good life?"

"Yes, Mom, it was."

———

After giving the female officer a quick description of the accident and leaving out a few pertinent details, Charlie hoped the woman would sympathize and do as she asked. "Would it be possible for someone to give me a ride?"

With the vehicle towed away and the ambulance carrying Ricard long gone, all that was left of the accident was Charlie and some bits of wreckage. Any evidence they'd carried in the SUV had been destroyed or scattered by the strong afternoon desert winds.

The officer tucked her pen in her shirt pocket and held the clipboard at her side. "Don't you have someone you can call?"

Charlie's mind flicked to Orr, the only remaining team member whose whereabouts were unknown. Did Angel hurt him? "I'm only here visiting. Could I get a lift to Vegas?" From there, she could arrange her own ride somehow to Area 51. No doubt that's exactly where Angel would be headed, too. Kellerman, Angel, and Allwood—all converging on the mysterious lab. She had to stop them. All of them.

The fighting and secrecy needed to end.

Today.

Officer Phillips reached the top of the embankment and handed Charlie another cell phone. "We found this on the ground about fifteen feet from the wreck. Still seems to be working. I'm assuming it belonged to the driver?"

Allwood's phone.

Charlie nodded. "That's right."

"Normally, we'd send it with the ambulance as part of the victim's belongings, but the EMTs have already left. I'm sure it'd be easier for you to take it to your friend rather than have it tied up at the station."

"Right. Sure." Without looking, she slid it into her pocket. "Which hospital?"

Phillips tucked his shirt in and wiped dirt off his pants. "Colorado River."

"Is that nearby?"

"Right off the highway in Needles."

The female officer, with a badge that read Garcia, said, "She's looking for a lift to Vegas."

Phillips nodded. "We can drive you to the hospital, but you'll have to find your own ride from there."

"Right." She couldn't waste time with a trip to the hospital and a long wait in the ER for a chance to talk to Ricard.

Garcia opened the driver's side door of their police vehicle and put the clipboard inside. "Are you coming, then?" She looked to Charlie.

Phillips strode out into the blocked traffic lane and picked up orange cones, handing them to another officer who carried them away.

Charlie shook her head. "I need to go to Vegas. I have a plane to catch."

"What about your friend?" Garcia tilted her head.

"I'll call his wife, and she can take care of him."

The officer's body grew rigid, and she placed her hands on her hips. "Could I have his phone, then?"

A beat-up Ford pick-up pulled onto the shoulder about fifteen feet in front of where Charlie stood. The window rolled down, and a familiar face looked back at her.

"Petty Officer Cutter," Commander Orr said. "Glad I finally found you. Let's go."

Her mouth gaped. She didn't know where he'd been, what had happened between him and Angel, or how he'd gotten a hold of a truck, but she didn't care.

Phillips, noticing the vehicle, stopped collecting cones and approached the driver. "Sir, you can't park here. You'll have to move along."

Despite the protests from Garcia about the cell phone in

Charlie's hand, she ran to the other side of the truck and climbed in.

"Just go, sir," she urged.

"Hey!" Phillips put a hand on his holster.

"Go!" Charlie banged on the dash.

Orr pressed on the gas, rear tires swerving, and rocketed onto the highway.

————

As they sped away, Charlie turned to look through the back window at the disappearing crash site. "You arrived just in time, Commander."

Orr appeared disheveled, which was unusual for him. Out of everyone at the office, aside from Angel, the commander never had anything out of place. But today? His hair was mussed, his shirt unbuttoned, and dust blanketed him.

"Where's Allwood and Ricard? What happened back there?"

"We had an accident. Allwood got away." She wasn't ready to spill the whole truth. Although she needed Orr for the ride to Area 51, she didn't want him to get in the way of what she needed to do. Orr was a by-the-book sort of Navy officer. Someone who wouldn't cut corners or break rules. She didn't have time for that.

"And Ricard? Is he all right?"

"I think so. He was awake when I saw him on the gurney."

Orr gave an acknowledging nod.

"What happened to you?" she asked.

With his gaze firmly fixed on the road, Orr's jaw tightened. "Demarco attacked me."

"What?"

"That bastard choked me out and left me for dead on the side of the road."

"My God." Angel had crossed a line she never thought he would.

"I'm going to throttle him with my bare hands when we catch up to him. Where do you think he is? Headed for Nellis?" The commander dodged a pair of Harleys cruising side by side and then the road opened up in front of them. He pressed on the gas, wringing as much power as he could out of the aging vehicle. "The authorities can pick up Kellerman, but Demarco? He's all mine."

Maybe Orr could break the rules after all. As long as she could keep her parentage a secret for today, her boss seemed willing to help in her pursuit.

"I think he's going to Area 51."

"Why do you think that?"

"He has Allwood. I think Angel wants to take him there for some kind of revenge." If Allwood was continuing his work at Area 51—the genetic modifications and 'improvements' Angel had described, it would make the most sense he'd want to destroy it.

Orr violently swerved the truck into another lane to avoid slamming into a car entering the highway. "How did he get a hold of Allwood?"

She thought a moment. "He hit us."

"Hell, Cutter, why didn't you tell me before?"

"Angel caused the wreck." She averted her gaze. "We spun out and went over the embankment."

"Shit."

"He took Allwood with him, and I'm sure that's where they'll go. Angel hates everything about him and knows he has a lab where the professor might be continuing his experiments."

"Charlie," the Commander said, using her given name for the first time, "we have to stop him."

"I know."

The scenery flew by in a blur. How many things would have to come together in order for her to end everything? She and Orr had no idea where Allwood's lab was located on base. But her gut told her all three of them—Kellerman, Allwood, and Angel would show up there. And they needed to arrive before Angel killed Allwood or destroyed his lab. There were answers she needed, questions she'd wanted to ask. She kicked herself for not having the courage to do it in front of Ricard.

For a long stretch of road, they traveled in silence.

The quiet only made her think more about her brother and the trouble he'd be in once the news broke out. How could she protect him? He needed to know the truth, and Allwood had to give it to her.

"How did you end up with this truck?" she asked.

"Some guy stopped to help me. I offered him cash for it. He accepted."

She tried to imagine someone willing to give up his truck to a stranger. "Did you pay him?"

"Ever heard of Cash App?"

She jerked. "Seriously?"

As the truck ate up the miles, they reviewed the facts about Angel, Allwood, the human experiments, everything.

But she stopped short of admitting her connection to Allwood. Orr would find out in time and telling him now would be a distraction. She was not the enemy here. Angel? He had nothing to lose. His whole focus since he'd traveled back in time had been to track down his number one enemy, Byron Allwood, and find his sister. Risa was lost to him, but Allwood? He was all too real. All too evil. And he'd landed right in Angel's lap. Years of anger, hatred, and frustration were about to be unleashed.

"Sir, we have to make it to Area 51 before he does something."

"Don't worry, Charlie, we will. I promise."

CHAPTER 18

AS KELLERMAN ARRIVED at the warehouse where the professor kept his work, he slowed the motorcycle and parked in the side lot where it would be less visible. The guards at the entrance to the secured area where the most secretive projects were housed let him by with barely a glance at his badge. They recognized him. For three years he'd worked with Allwood and passed through the same gates every morning. Even after he'd taken the transfer to NCIS-A, he made occasional trips to Nevada to report in person about his findings.

The lab would be closed at this time of day. He judged the angle of the sun—maybe two more hours of daylight. But he wouldn't be leaving the facility once he entered.

His stomach fluttered.

He brushed his thumb across his access card. The professor should have confiscated it when the lieutenant had taken on his new assignment. But it had been easier to let him keep it. No questions asked when he returned for one-on-one meetings to transfer intel to Allwood.

He chose an entrance at the back of the facility—closest to the professor's office and nearest the locked room where the experiment in progress lived. The one he'd helped bring to fruition through his sacrifice and cunning. They wouldn't be as far along on it if he hadn't collected samples and crafted some of the software to reveal the formula's building blocks.

Would they have changed the code since he left last year?

He punched in the numbers and hoped.

The metallic click told him the professor had been sloppy in his security procedures. The combination should've been changed every three months. But how many times had he reminded Allwood to do it? The professor didn't care much about rules and regulations. He only wanted to be left alone to continue his work. He'd relied on Kellerman to keep the security auditors out of his hair, but never thought to select a replacement.

His mistake.

The door buzzed. He entered and headed upstairs to the room that held their greatest achievement: a time machine.

After waving his badge in front of the card scanner, Kellerman entered the dark room and flipped on a switch. Fluorescent lights lit up the space. The warmth of the room meant it hadn't been long since Allwood's best scientists had occupied it.

A large organic orb took up half the room. It rested in a metal stand. A wall of floor-to-ceiling plexiglass separated the machine from the row of computers and equipment on the opposite wall. Humidity steamed up the inside of the glass. One of the first things they'd had to figure out was the level of dampness that kept the orb from disintegrating, but also kept the organic material from crumbling. He was sure the last few samples he'd collected from North Dakota helped finalize the formula. No need to wait for the translations any longer. Who cared if Allwood wanted to run a few more simulations?

The lieutenant stood there for a moment staring at the object. When he'd hopped on the motorcycle and zoomed down the highway, he'd had a very focused mind. To reach the machine and disappear to another time—like the professor had promised—had been his only goal. With the reveal that Charlie was his daughter, he'd begun to doubt Allwood would follow through.

But was he really ready to leave everything he knew for life in a time period long past?

He placed his palm on the glass and dipped his head.

What did he have left in this time?

Ricard, Orr, and Charlie knew the truth—he'd been deceiving them. His work at NCIS-A was over. His clearance would be pulled. He'd never be able to work in intelligence again, which meant not even the professor could fix things. With Charlie in the picture, and Armas, too, he was only an assistant who'd aided Allwood in his quest. An easily replaceable assistant.

His hand turned into a fist.

With determination, he headed for the computer that controlled the pod. He knew how to program it, as he'd helped build the code based on instructions from Allwood. According to the professor, his wife had crafted the formula for the original machines, and he had created the inner workings that directed it. With unfamiliar twenty-first century tech at his disposal, the professor had handed over that work to Kellerman and others who came before him and, instead, focused his time on growing his sources of funding for the project.

But with the arrival of Armas in a pod from the past, Kellerman wondered at the truth of Allwood's abilities. How much of the machine was truly the professor's work?

The screen came to life. Kellerman navigated to the command program. With trembling fingers he typed in his time destination—not so far back that he'd be stuck in a primitive time with little hope for survival, but not so modern that he'd ever be tracked down or noticed.

A hatch appeared in the side of the pod and hissed open.

———

Demarco slowed their speed to avoid unwanted attention and kept a careful eye on his prisoner. He wouldn't put it past the man to jump out of a moving vehicle traveling at eighty miles an hour. He'd kept pace with traffic for the last hundred miles or so. The cops were probably already out looking for a stolen vehicle, and who knows what Charlie told the police once help arrived.

His gut twisted.

It couldn't be helped.

He had to choose Allwood over her.

It was always going to be that way.

To bring Charlie into his world and share what he'd seen and suffered because of this man came with risks. She'd been sympathetic, kind, and loving. When he'd climbed into the machine all those years ago, he hadn't expected to have the love of a woman in his life. He'd chosen his path. A lonely one. A path he'd intended only for himself. Then he'd met her.

The temptation had been strong to end his quest and forget about everything: his family, the horrible experiments, the loss of his sister. One part of him longed for it—to have a wife, children, a regular life. The dream reminded him so much of home on the farm his heart ached for it. A time when everything had been simpler. But then he knew he'd never completely forget, and his obsession would always haunt him.

After he eradicated Allwood and his experiments and everything was known, Charlie would loathe him. If she didn't already after the way he'd abandoned her at the accident scene. She must know he was responsible. Perhaps he'd shut the door on his dream the minute he chose to ram the SUV.

"Where are we going?" For tens of miles Allwood had remained silent, but now he'd finally opened up.

The sound of his voice grated on Demarco. If only the man knew the level of hatred inside, he'd stop drawing attention to himself.

Demarco snorted a breath through his nose. The 'professor' didn't deserve an answer.

"My arm, it's broken." The older man held it awkwardly in his lap. "Are you going to do something about it?"

"Shut up." Demarco spied a police car parked under an overpass and slowed the car. "When we drive up to the gates, you're going to act as if everything is normal. I'm your security. That's what you'll tell them."

"They won't let you on base without a badge."

"It's your job to make sure they do."

"I can't make someone break the rules."

"All you've ever done is break the rules, Allwood." Demarco pushed a thumb into the professor's leg wound.

Allwood let out a strangled cry.

"You will get me on that base." He gritted his teeth.

"You're an animal. A lunatic who should've been put down instead of caged. But your sister begged me to spare you." Allwood spat out his words. "Little did she know that decision would ruin our plans and destroy everything we'd built."

The speeding landscape around them blurred. Demarco's vision tunneled. So the only reason he'd lived, the only reason he'd been spared in Allwood's lair that day was because of Risa?

"If you truly believe that, then you'd do anything this 'animal' asks." A dark place grew in his heart. "Because this animal is dangerous and unpredictable."

The exit appeared. He swerved off the highway.

Allwood cried out when his mangled arm pressed against the door.

Although the professor had a charisma that drew people to him and a commanding presence, Demarco saw right through it to the person inside. A petty, shallow man who never cared about anyone but himself. The kind of man who would do almost anything to save his own ass.

If Allwood couldn't find a way to pass him through the security check point, Demarco would have to get creative.

———

Kellerman stared at the pod. Although he'd dreamed of becoming a time traveler, he never thought the day would arrive. Everything he'd worked for, every task the professor had assigned him, no matter how difficult, had been worth it.

Having a top secret security clearance meant he had to become good at lying or at least avoiding the truth, and the professor had only encouraged him in the deception game. They'd been a team. Kellerman had become his right-hand man and knew more than the high-ranking officers and politicians who funded the research.

But look how Allwood treated him after everything he'd sacrificed. Instead of bringing him closer in, the professor had begun pushing him away. Armas's arrival had been the first noticeable shift. The existence of the boy in this time increased Allwood's eagerness to complete the pods. It was the proof he'd needed that his wife had survived her trip to the distant past. The conversation shifted from the professor needing a knowledgeable companion to travel with him through time to the hope for a reunion with his wife and child. Kellerman became an after-thought.

He wouldn't take it anymore.

He wasn't some obedient dog who'd do anything Allwood asked.

All his decisions would now be about what was best for him. What *he* wanted. What *he* dreamed of.

The lieutenant spun around and navigated to a folder on the desktop. One that nobody noticed. A program he'd written months ago when he felt the professor slipping away and focusing more on his wife than on him.

He inserted the hidden code into the system and started the countdown. In ten minutes, after the machine had carried him to his new time and new life, all of the team's work would be erased. The formula they'd been working on for years would disappear. The bioelectric circuit design and the software he'd perfected to interface with them would no longer exist.

He smiled to himself when he'd finished.

Let the professor see how important he'd been to the work.

How much Allwood needed him.

After a few seconds of watching the timer count down, he rose, opened the plexiglass door, and closed it behind him.

The machine had a strange smell—damp but also intensely green, like a freshly mowed lawn. He climbed through the hatch. Beneath his feet the soft, organic surface clung to him. He touched the seat. The cool goo vibrated, which was unpleasant. But his travel should only last a few minutes, and then he'd be free of this time, free of the life he no longer wanted.

He thought fleetingly of his brother and sister and what they'd think. His family would mourn for a time, but the military would probably claim he'd been lost in some kind of accident. They'd receive his benefits and probably move on. And he? He would be living the life he should've had. He'd be in a place where his knowledge and insight would be worshipped.

After he sat down and strapped in, he pulled the organic restraint taut against his chest and clicked it into place.

The hatch hissed closed.

Kellerman took a deep breath, and his heart raced. Inky blackness enveloped him.

Allwood had never mentioned anything about the dark.

The machine began to spin, and as it did, bioluminescence lit up the interior. The minimal controls were visible, as were the walls that protected him from the time waves he'd pass through.

He gripped the restraint, closed his eyes, and waited.

CHAPTER 19

FROM INSIDE THE LAB, if someone happened to be present, the machine behind the plexiglass spun and spun and spun until it was a blur. A loud whooshing sound filled the small space that soon became deafening.

Then a computer screen lit up with a red warning: *Danger*.

The machine continued to spin. If someone looked closely, maybe it tilted slightly off its axis, maybe its green goo began to melt, and maybe the material that was supposed to withstand the rigors of time travel wasn't quite the right formula.

Maybe.

The whoosh turned into a whine.

The rounded sides of the machine pressed inward, creating an oblong shape. Then, instead of disappearing, the object imploded splattering green goo mixed with red onto the clear walls.

Silence filled the room.

Green and red chunks wetly dripped down the clear walls.

The computer's warning disappeared, Kellerman's countdown continued, and within minutes everything had been erased.

CHAPTER 20

LESS THAN A HALF-MILE from the highway exit, the road to Groom Lake turned to gravel. Demarco slowed the vehicle. With the sun low in the sky, strange shadows created dark patches that hid potholes and dips. Anyone traveling down this road would think it abandoned and turn around for the safety of the busy highway and the bright lights of Las Vegas in the distance. But Demarco and his passenger wouldn't be turning around. No, they would be following the road until it ended at their destination. No other option existed.

"Were you going to meet Kellerman at your lab?" The why of the lieutenant's mad dash from the pod landing site stood out as still unexplained in his mind. What prompted Kellerman to blow his cover? "Did he contact you while we were at the hospital? Tell you anything?" He glanced over at the man nursing his painful arm. "Where's your phone?"

"I lost it when you crashed into us back there." Allwood grimaced when the car bounced over a dip in the road.

"Hope you didn't hurt your friends. That girl looked pretty banged up."

Demarco's mind returned to Charlie—the blood, the startled look on her face when he'd fled the scene with his captive. His vision fuzzed out. But it was for the best if she finally saw him for who he was: a man full of hate, a man obsessed with revenge. He had no room for anything else. This was who he was. His life had been distilled down to the actions he was about to take. After he achieved his goal, he didn't care what happened to him. He had nothing left in this time, nothing to hold him back from his plan.

"Where's Kellerman?" He turned the conversation back to Allwood's lackey and NCIS-A's mole. "Did he think you'd hide him? Keep him safe? Or was he going to be another subject for your experiments? Were you going to cut him open? Inject him with something? Alter his DNA for your own sick fun?"

"We're almost there." Allwood stared straight ahead.

Demarco noticed two faint lights in the distance. Not what he expected at a high security military facility. But perhaps the scaled down lighting helped with the hidden nature of the base and the secrets it held. Why draw attention? The badly maintained road, the minimal lighting—so far everything screamed: old, broken down, no longer used.

His headlights caught the white of a reflective sign with faded red lettering:

WARNING
Restricted Area
It is unlawful to enter this area without
permission of the Installation Commander

Sec. 21, Internal Security Act of 1950; 50 U.S.C. 797
While on this Installation all personnel and
the property under their control are subject
to search
Use of deadly force authorized

"What if I told you I have a working machine in my lab, a machine that would allow you to join your sister?"

The unexpected words hit the special agent like a concussive blast after an explosion. Demarco's grip tightened on the steering wheel. There was a chance to find Risa? "I don't believe you." But his mind raced at the suggestion. Reunited with his sister? He thought about what she must've gone through without him—the loneliness, the confusion, and the physical strain of such a massive time jump. Then there was Armas. She'd given up her child to one of these pods with the hope he'd find safety, or family, or Allwood. He wished he knew. Had she intended to join her son? Or had something happened to her?

"You should. It's all very real. I've been working for decades on the formula. When I found the Voynich manuscript on the internet, I knew it was Risa's work. I knew I could rebuild the machines even with a partial formula. The internet? Pretty amazing thing. When I figured out what it could do, even back in the late 1990s, something told me to search for answers, look for her. I knew Risa would find a way to communicate with me. But who knew she would speak from a place centuries earlier." The older man couldn't hide the scowl on his face.

"And Kellerman? What was his role in all of this, if you found Risa's work?"

"The formula was incomplete. I needed samples, and when my followers began to arrive—in the time I had selected before you interfered—I needed someone who could blend in and collect them for me without being recognized. Kellerman has been a great help to me in the last year. I have a machine waiting. That's why the senator was visiting. She wanted to see the culmination of twenty years of work."

A flare of adrenaline fired in Demarco's brain. "Why would you give me the chance, when you could use it and travel to any time you wanted?"

"I know you hate me," Allwood said and pushed his body back into his seat. "I know you blame me for everything that has happened to your family. There's no way you'll let me walk out of this alive." The professor made an odd noise in his throat. "If you leave me in this time and allow me to live, I'll give you the chance to be reunited with your sister."

An empty feeling hollowed out Demarco's stomach. "It's all your fault, so why wouldn't I blame you?"

"I'll give up everything, destroy my work. No one will ever hear from me again. I'll end it all tonight."

Demarco knew deep down Allwood was a liar and a charlatan. But the desire to rescue his sister and save her from a lifetime of isolation, such as he'd experienced, was strong. It tugged at him with a force he didn't think possible. Every moment he'd spent with Risa on the farm flashed through his mind. She'd been determined, intelligent, but also kind. A kindness that had led her to Allwood in the first place. She believed his words and joined in his passion. She'd made a mistake, and she had paid for it with the loss of everything she ever knew, even the loss of her child. The suffering she must had endured. He couldn't bear it. What if Allwood spoke the truth?

"Take me to the machine."

————

After another ten minutes of driving down the gravel road, they approached the guard shack standing outside rusted fencing. Although a spiral of barbed wire ran the length of it, the age of the base showed. Or was that intentional to keep prying eyes away?

Demarco turned off his headlights.

A young airman in BDUs motioned for him to roll down his window, another man in uniform hung back by the guard shack and gripped his rifle.

Demarco pressed on the electric window button. A warm, dusty wind blew inside.

"Badges?" The airman peeked in the RAV4. "Oh, professor, I didn't recognize the vehicle. How are you this evening, sir?"

The professor nodded and smiled a tight smile. "Fine, fine."

The airman gave Demarco a quizzical look.

"He's my security—from NCIS." Allwood nodded at Demarco who flashed his identification.

"Something up?" The airman signaled to his partner who headed for the gate and entered a code. The chain-link shuddered and then slowly rolled to the right on rusted wheels to open.

"Some sort of silly threat." The professor used his uninjured arm to shrug. "All I know is the base commander called me this afternoon, assigned this guy from Nellis, and now he has to follow me wherever I go. Irritating, but I can play along."

Demarco kept his face impassive. He wanted to press on the gas and fly through the open gate. Allwood's lab was somewhere behind this fence. He'd waited half a dozen years for this moment, and he wasn't about to let his impatience take over and destroy his chances. Besides, if the professor had told him the truth, there might be a way to rescue his sister. Maybe that was the only avenue for him anyway. What did he have left in this time? Nothing. He'd burned every bridge and ruined every relationship with his actions today. Even if he came out of this unscathed, he'd have to start all over in a new place with a different name. Could he handle that again? He'd barely kept his sanity when he'd done it the first time.

The airman stepped back and waved. "Come on through."

"Thanks," said Allwood. "I'll have to give you the tour sometime."

The young Air Force guard raised his eyebrows. "Really? That'd be cool."

Demarco crept through the gate.

———

At night, Area 51 gave off an eerie feel. The lighting was minimal, the signage almost non-existent, and row after row of identical warehouse buildings indicated a lot more secret research could exist here than Allwood's.

"Your sister was truly remarkable, you know."

The professor appeared more relaxed than he had the entire trip, which set Demarco on edge. "Where's your lab?" Everything looked the same, nothing stood out to him—wide, low greenish-brown buildings with white doors on the front and sides. Depending on Allwood to find what he needed made him uneasy.

"The code—in the Voynich manuscript and in our machines—was something she created." Allwood stared out the window and watched as they passed by building after building. "Did you know that?"

"No." It ticked him off that Allwood teased him with facts about his sister. It had been so long since he'd seen her climb into a pod and disappear, he could barely remember her features, much less the intelligence she displayed. His memories tied back to her collection of plants, her drawings in her sketchbook, her mischievous smile when she bested him in class. Less than two years younger, but so obviously smarter than him in many ways even at a young age.

"We left notes for each other at the stone bridge, and she attempted to teach me. She saw it as a way for our people to communicate secretively. I only had a minimal grasp before your thugs showed up, and we had to escape."

Demarco grunted.

The stone bridge had been a landmark between their village and the ruins of an earlier time. Their parents had forbidden them to go any further than the bridge. The ruins held untold dangers from their ancestors that could threaten their way of life. That information had been passed down from grandparents and great-grandparents and great-great-grandparents. The warning went so far back nobody knew who had started it or why. But they all obeyed...until Byron

Allwood came along preaching his nonsense about transformation and becoming something more than human. Better than human.

"I loved her for her mind, her brilliance," the professor continued. "For things her family never noticed, never praised. She was beyond her time, beyond all of you—even me. I can see that now. When we were separated in time, and I found myself alone, without her, without our people—well, I'm sure you can understand how disorienting it was."

Demarco gritted his teeth. He remembered all right. He thought he was going to travel to a distant place on earth, and instead he made a decision that changed the course of his entire life. Forever. No going back. No fixing things. His parents wouldn't be born for hundreds of years. He had no idea if decisions he made in this time would affect their existence. His head hurt at the thought.

"I wished I'd been a better student. That would have made things so much easier." Allwood brushed dust off his clothes with his good hand. "Until your team found someone who could translate the manuscript, I had to rely only on my memory and the few bits of code she'd taught me." Allwood gently lifted the wrist of his broken arm and set it in a different position on his lap. He sucked air between his teeth. "Where did you find your translator? I'd hired several over the years, and they'd all failed. Told me translation was impossible. That dozens of people over hundreds of years hadn't been able to break it. Then, within weeks, your newest team member, the young lady in the accident I believe, managed to figure it out. I wonder how that was possible?"

Charlie.

Demarco imagined her earnest face when she'd listened to his story. The first time he'd shared it with anyone. Why did it have to be her? Why did she have to be the one? Anyone but her. The one person who could translate the text, who could uncover the whole scheme, and who'd revealed his sister's fate and her role in everything.

"You can stop here." Allwood pointed at an unlit building like all the other buildings, except this one had a familiar yellow-and-black motorcycle parked alongside it.

Kellerman.

"This is the building you want. The lab is inside." The older man straightened up in his seat. "Behind those doors is the way to reunite with your sister and put this all behind you."

Demarco parked, turned off the engine, and decided what he would do.

CHAPTER 21

Miles away from Allwood and Demarco...

CHARLIE NAVIGATED USING her cell phone. Surprisingly, it had been as easy as typing 'Area 51' into her mapping app to find a route to the military site. As the sky grew darker, though, identifying the landmarks they needed to take the right exit became harder. "I can't believe someone uploaded a picture of the entrance." She held up her phone so the commander could see a clear photo of a chain-link gate manned by guards. "I thought it was a highly classified, well-protected base."

Orr shrugged. "Everyone knows where the NSA is located, but you don't see random conspiracy theorists driving through the gates."

Charlie's mind flashed to I-95 and the familiar turn-off to her stepfather's work place. "True."

Orr turned on the headlights, and the reflective lane striping lit up. "You think Allwood would help Demarco get on the base if he knew what Demarco was thinking?"

"Good question." How would he make it through security without a badge or having his name on an access list?

Luckily for her, Commander Orr had connections through his father who'd worked at the site decades ago before his disappearance. When they'd decided on their destination, he'd made a couple of phone calls, and in less than an hour, they had everything they needed to enter the site. Some admiral or other had arranged it. Charlie had no idea Orr's family background and the clout their small office, NCIS-A, could wield when needed.

Orr gave her a quick glance. "Could Allwood want him to reach his lab?"

She smoothed her hair back from her face. "Are you suggesting the professor might be setting up a trap?" Her mouth went dry.

"Maybe."

A directional sign lit up under the glare of their headlights. "We turn off at the next exit." Her stomach quivered. They were only a few miles away, had no weapons, and would arrive completely out of their element. They'd be right in Allwood's backyard. It wasn't a good idea. In fact, it was a terrible idea.

"If you were trapped in a car with Demarco and knew he wanted to kill you, what would you do to save your own ass?" the commander asked.

Orr's speculation turned her mind in a different direction. If they didn't intercede, lives could be at stake. She thought of the woman in the hospital who had been murdered by a man she trusted. Allwood had convinced her to climb into a pod and travel through time. She had depended on him for everything, and he'd turned on her. If

Allwood could do that to someone who'd trusted him completely, what could he do to someone he hated? Someone who'd chased him through time? Someone who would do anything to eradicate the man he blamed for everything bad in his life?

As they approached the exit, a decaying white mobile home a hundred yards from the highway appeared in their headlights. What poor misbegotten soul had decided to build a life for himself so far outside Las Vegas and miles from any civilization?

It dawned on her at that moment how far away they were from people and police and safety. Maybe it was one of the reasons Demarco wanted to end it here. Away from prying eyes. A score could be settled, and no one would be the wiser. Demarco was clever enough and angry enough he'd find a way to hide what he'd done. A secret base in the middle of the desert with incredibly high security? No one would interrupt him. No one would stop him. No one would get in his way.

Her armpits grew damp.

Charlie expanded her map in order to see more clearly what terrain lay beyond the exit to Area 51.

Orr turned off the highway.

"Do you think you can drive faster?" she asked.

"This road looks rough." Orr kicked on the brights.

The reality of what they were about to do settled heavily inside her. Her gaze bounced from one side of the road to the other—only sand and dirt and empty nothingness surrounded them on both sides. "I think we're running out of time."

Orr glanced over at her, gave a nod, and pressed on the

gas. The old truck lurched forward and carried them further into the desert.

———

Demarco followed the injured Allwood to the back of the warehouse, where a dimly lit door awaited them. As they passed by the motorcycle, the special agent touched the engine with the back of his hand. Still warm. Kellerman had arrived not too long ago. Allwood didn't even give it a glance. He had no idea Kellerman had stolen it to put miles between himself and his former co-workers.

What had the young lieutenant discovered that had sent him on the run and exposed his subterfuge?

Demarco prepared himself for the possibility that Kellerman might be inside the lab waiting for his boss. A pre-arranged meeting? An opportunity to change their plans now that Kellerman's cover had been blown? Or was it something else? Information obtained from the dead woman in the hospital or something that had yet to be revealed to the NCIS-A team?

"Remember who has the upper hand here, Allwood." Demarco focused his attention on the wounded man who limped as he walked and held his arm close to his body. Did Allwood know this day would come? Had Allwood suspected he would follow him into the unknown, climb inside a pod, and join him in time traveling madness?

The older man paused, keeping his back to Demarco, and said, "I'm only interested in both of us getting what we want."

They approached the door. A keypad was affixed on the

wall next to it. Allwood pressed a series of numbers, and the door beeped twice.

Demarco wished he still had his gun or his taser—both useful weapons. But he'd known a time when neither of those things existed, and he'd had to use other means to control his enemies. If Kellerman were waiting behind the door, he needed to be ready.

Allwood pulled on the knob. It opened. In the blink of an eye, Demarco slid an arm across Allwood's throat, pulled the man close, and whispered in his ear, "Nice and slow. We wouldn't want anyone to get hurt."

Allwood grunted and slowed his movements.

Demarco noticed lights were on inside, which told him Kellerman wouldn't be lying in wait. Too exposed. Too visible.

The professor's body tensed. "Are you going to let go now?" he croaked. "I'm offering you everything you ever wanted, and this is how you treat me?"

Demarco wanted to crush the man's throat, shut him up forever. "Not everything." He swallowed the bile that rose in his throat, released his hold on the man, and thrust him forward into the building. It would be so easy to snap his neck. He'd done it before to men stronger and more capable than Allwood. Or he could find a sharp object inside and stab him in the heart. And he'd do it without remorse, without guilt, without a single thought in his mind but vengeance.

They entered a small vestibule—plain, utilitarian, with no indications of what sort of work went on inside. A stairway to the left led up a flight of metal stairs, and several closed doors spanned the length of the white, unadorned wall in front of them.

To gain back some control, Demarco bit the inside of his cheek.

He craved to know more about the secrets inside this place. If he gave in to his baser instincts, he'd kill Allwood before he learned what had been hidden behind security codes and military protection. What vile experiments had he conducted?

Allwood headed for a door on the right. "This way."

"I want to see it all. Everything. I want you to walk me through every square inch of this space and show me what the military has been funding all these years. With this time's technology and the government's money, I can't even imagine how twisted your research has become."

"Twisted?" Allwood spat out. "Is that what you think? My life-saving therapies—"

"Life-saving? Is that what you call horrible disfigurement and manipulated DNA?" Demarco planted himself on the hard concrete floor. His muscles quivered. "A perfectly healthy human being reduced to a freak without knowing the long-term implications of your experiments? What did you promise the poor victims who came to you for help?"

"People came to me because no one else cared. I was the only one who attempted to improve their lives, make them something better. Your kind would leave them to suffer."

"Risa needed no improvement."

"I didn't do anything to anyone that I didn't try out on myself. Your sister saw what could be achieved and begged me to fix her. She knew she could be so much more with a few tweaks—smarter, stronger, better."

"A few tweaks? I saw what you did to her. You disfigured her."

"I made her more beautiful."

"She was perfect the way she was."

"She didn't see it that way," Allwood said. "And who are you to tell her what and who she should be? That was one of the reasons she ran away and came to me. I could see her potential. I could see what she could become. She trusted me completely and was involved in every step, every surgery, every genetic manipulation."

"Stop." Demarco gripped the back of Allwood's neck. "I can't listen to your lies anymore."

The older man shook off his hand. "If only she were here now and you could speak to her, she'd tell you the truth."

A muffled sound echoed down to the vestibule from the floor above.

"Someone's here," Allwood whispered.

Was the professor surprised or merely a good actor?

Allwood peered up the dark steps. "No one should be in the building this late. Unless—"

Demarco's assumptions about Kellerman and why he'd fled for the lab dispersed in his mind like falling snow into dry air. "Unless what?"

"Unless that fool betrayed me." The older man shuffled toward the stairs. "I told him it wasn't ready, but he was so eager. So stupidly eager."

"What wasn't ready?" It made no difference to Demarco if he saw the upstairs of Allwood's lab first or the downstairs. If something upstairs made the man grow concerned about what Kellerman may be up to, Demarco was perfectly fine following him and finding out more.

Everything was going to end tonight. He would make sure nobody else would ever follow Allwood's path, rebuild his discoveries, or move ahead on any of it. Then he could climb inside one of those machines, take one last trip back in time, and destroy the Voynich manuscript before it could ever be discovered and translated. The work, the partial formula, every little scrap of the evil machine had to be destroyed. Demarco only trusted himself to make sure it would happen. He might be trapped in a more primitive time for the rest of his life, but at least he would be with his sister. He could find a way to make her trust him again, love him again. They could save each other from the loneliness and aguish that came with being a time traveler.

The professor took each step with care. When his injured left leg pushed up on a step, he hissed between his teeth. "Help me, you idiot. Kellerman is about to ruin everything."

Demarco brought his shoulder up under Allwood's good arm and helped him climb the stairs. When they reached the second floor, Allwood pointed to a dark hallway lit only by a few downward pointing lights.

The professor untangled himself from Demarco and hobbled down the hall. "The lab's down there. Hurry!"

Although his gut told him not to trust, Demarco's curiosity burned. If Kellerman wanted to access the room Allwood was leading him to, then it must contain something important. That traitor had shown his true colors back in Lake Havasu—his loyalty was only to himself. He'd known from Kellerman's first day at NCIS-A there was something off, but Orr had seemed thrilled to have someone with his tech skills on the team. Now it looked as if the commander had chosen poorly.

Allwood breathed heavily but seemed to have found a second wind. When he opened up his stride a little too much his wounded leg collapsed under him.

Demarco caught him before he went down. "Easy, old man, you don't want that leg wound to bleed worse than it already is." Besides, if the professor passed out, how would he access the room the man seemed so eager to reach? He again offered Allwood his shoulder in support.

With the help of Demarco, Allwood neared a door that looked like all the other doors in the warehouse. No markings on it. No indication of what went on behind it. Maybe as a way to control the secrecy?

"You need to help me with my badge." Allwood's broken arm was useless and the other was slung across Demarco's back and shoulders.

A white card reader, like the ones at the Washington Navy Yard, hung on the wall. "Where is it?" He patted the pockets of Allwood's suit jacket.

A strange whirring sound emanated from behind it.

"Goddammit, it's too late." Allwood snarled.

"Where's your badge?" Demarco snapped. If Kellerman was on the other side of that door, he wanted to know what he was up to. Who cared if it was 'too late'?

"My inside pocket."

Demarco felt inside the lining of the jacket.

"Hurry." The professor stomped his good foot. "We don't have much time."

"Got it." Demarco pulled out Allwood's badge and waved it in front of the card reader.

A metal ker-thunk sounded indicating the door was now open, followed by a muffled explosion.

They burst through the door.

Demarco's eyes landed first on the blood-and-goo streaked Plexiglass in one corner of the room. "What the hell?"

Allwood freed himself from Demarco's support and grabbed for a roller chair next to a bank of desktop computers. "The idiot. Why couldn't he wait?"

Demarco pointed at the mess behind the clear protective wall. "Is that Kellerman? Was that a pod?"

The professor nodded dumbly and lowered himself into the chair, staring at the screens. "He destroyed everything. All my work."

The special agent approached the enclosed area that had housed his former co-worker inside a pod. "Why did it blow up?" A chunk of goo slowly slid to the floor. Was that a body part partially coated in more green gunk? *Oh, Kellerman, what did you do?*

Allwood tapped furiously on a keyboard. "I don't think I can stop it. Do you want to see your sister again? Help me."

Demarco turned away from the sordid scene and focused his attention on the professor. "What do you mean?"

"All of my work. That stupid lieutenant of yours must've created a hidden instruction to destroy the formula I've been working on." Allwood typed while lines of code disappeared in front of their eyes. "The formula to build another machine. If we can't stop it, neither of us is going anywhere."

CHAPTER 22

AS DEMARCO APPROACHED THE COMPUTER, his stomach hardened. "Wait, you were going to put me in that machine, weren't you? The one that exploded and killed Kellerman?"

Allwood focused on the lines of codes in front of him as if Demarco didn't even exist. The older man was so intent on his precious research, he didn't even realize he'd exposed his sinister plan.

"You snake." Demarco's hands curved as if they were strangling the professor's neck. "I never should've trusted you."

"All of my work. Ruined." Allwood's hands shook as he navigated the screen with a wireless mouse. "Years of experiments, trials, formulas. That bastard." With an angry grunt, he picked up the keyboard and smashed it on the desk.

Demarco spun the chair around. "You were going to kill me."

The professor's eyes were fever bright, and he clung to

his seat with his good hand. "And you weren't planning the same?" He raised an eyebrow.

A mirthless laugh escaped the special agent. "All these years, and you are the exactly same person. You haven't changed at all."

"Neither have you." The older man kicked at Demarco with his good leg and turned back around. "Let me save what I can." He reached down and pulled the cord from the wall to permanently shut off the computer and whatever program had been operating. "My team will have to sort through this disaster in the morning. We'll find a way to rebuild."

Allwood thought he'd return to business as usual? After he'd murdered a woman, lured Kellerman to his untimely demise, and who knows what else? Even though Demarco wanted nothing more than to follow through on his dark thoughts and strangle the life out of his nemesis, the blinging of a phone caught his attention.

Kellerman's phone.

The young lieutenant had left it on the desk before he'd foolishly tried to escape in an experimental pod. Guess he thought he wouldn't need it in whatever time he'd chosen as his destination.

Maybe there would be a clue on it that would expose Allwood's sick plans. Could there be more in this massive warehouse than Genesis Machine pieces and parts? Was he still conducting human experiments and DNA manipulation?

He reached for it.

Allwood beat him to it. "Not so fast." In a flash he'd typed a six-digit code with one hand and unlocked the phone. He must've seen a look of surprise on Demarco's face. "You think

I wouldn't know how to access his phone? Nobody works for me unless they are willing to share everything."

The screen displayed an email that Kellerman must've had open before he'd made his fateful decision to enter the pod.

As he read the email message, Allwood's face paled. His gaze slid to Demarco. "Would your translator's name be Charlene Cutter? The one who so cleverly deciphered the Voynich text?"

Demarco's mind froze. Why was this lunatic bringing up Charlie? What did Kellerman dig up about her? "Leave her out of this."

A slow smile spread across the older man's face. "Oh, you don't know then, do you?"

"Know what?" The gleam in Allwood's eyes was evil. The hair rose on the back of Demarco's neck. He grabbed at the phone. "What does it say?"

"Charlene and a brother." Allwood's face beamed. "I didn't know she'd given birth to twins."

"I don't understand." Demarco's adrenaline spiked. The truth had been right in front of him, and he'd ignored it. The unusual capabilities. The odd connection to the manuscript. He took a step backward. "No, it can't be."

"Yes," Allwood said. "Charlene Cutter is my daughter."

CHAPTER 23

AS ORR SLOWED DOWN, the truck headlights played across the entrance to Area 51. It looked identical to the photo online: a chain link fence topped with razor wire, a simple guard shack, and a few external lights. With the sun completely set, night had swept across the desert, enveloping them in total blackness. The sight of bright lights and civilization—even if it was high-security civilization—brought an unexpected release of all tension in Charlie's body.

"Now we'll find out if my contacts did as promised," Commander Orr said as two uniformed airmen approached.

One of the men rested a hand on his sidearm and stayed a good fifteen feet away from the truck. The other tapped on the window glass.

Orr rolled it down.

"I'm sorry, sir, this is a secure site. We'll have to ask you to turn around."

Orr flashed his NCIS-A badge. "I was told you'd be expecting me."

The airmen's eyebrows shot up, he stepped back, and

gave a quick salute. "Yes, Commander. I'm sorry, sir. We didn't expect you to arrive"—he eyeballed the junker the high-ranking officer drove—"in a truck."

"Stand down, airman."

The young man dropped his salute and gave a hand signal to his partner to back off. "It'll take us a minute to open the gate. Never seen it so busy this late in the day."

"Oh?" Orr tilted his head. "You've had other visitors tonight?"

The other airman opened the gate and waved at Orr and Charlie to move forward.

"One of our civilian scientists. But he does that some-times—shows up at night. Whatever he's working on must be really important."

Orr nodded. "Sounds like it. I appreciate your help tonight, airman."

"Sir." The guard dipped his chin and stepped back from the truck.

Orr pushed on the gas and crept through the gate.

As they left the two guards behind, Charlie looked over her shoulder and watched the gate grow smaller. "You made that look so easy."

Orr shrugged. "It was."

"I thought for sure they'd notice my hands." She held them up to show the commander how much they shook.

"No worries, Petty Officer Cutter. I have this under control. All we have to do now is find the right building." He scanned the multiple rows of old military warehouses that lined the road.

"Should we have asked back there?" Charlie jerked a thumb.

"Ask where Allwood did his experiments? That might've made them suspicious of our motives."

"Maybe." She bit her lip. "But I'm worried it will take us forever to find them by ourselves, and I don't think we have a lot of time."

"I know what Demarco's vehicle looks like. He wouldn't expect anyone to follow him here, so I doubt he hid it from view."

Charlie's phone rang.

Orr's eyebrows furrowed. "Dr. Stern?"

Her stomach dropped. "It's my brother." *Chad.* He'd returned her call at the worst possible time. But she couldn't put off talking to him. His life could be in danger if she waited much longer to share the distressing news. "Could you pull over?"

"What?" He lifted his foot off the gas.

"I need to talk to my brother—privately." Her body flashed hot and cold. This might be her only opportunity to tell Chad the truth before everyone knew.

"Cutter—"

"Please, sir. I wouldn't ask unless it was important."

"We don't have time for this. I'm sure your brother can wait."

The phone rang again. The sound made her grit her teeth. "Sir."

"Hang up."

"What?"

Orr reached for her phone. "Hang up. You can call your brother when all of this is over."

Charlie leaned away and quickly answered it. Her breathing accelerated. "Chad, did you get my text?"

Even though her brother was thousands of miles away in Spain, his voice came through clearly, "I talked to Mom."

Her stomach bottomed out. He knew. "I'm sorry."

Orr grunted. She'd defied him, and he wasn't happy about it.

"What do you have to be sorry about? You didn't know anything either. We both were kept in the dark." He let out a sigh. "What I don't understand is, why would you tell Mom we were in danger? People take DNA tests all the time and find out family secrets. This doesn't change how I feel about Dad. Who cares?"

Charlie swallowed and gave a quick glance in Orr's direction. She had to warn him. "It's the truth. Believe me. I wouldn't say that if I didn't mean it."

"Spit it out, Charlie. I don't have time for your nonsense."

"When everyone finds out, both of our lives are going to change."

"Why? Who is this Byron Allwood guy?"

Orr braked the truck. He pointed across the road at a dark warehouse that looked like all the other dark warehouses they'd passed. "There's the car and the motorcycle Kellerman stole."

Dammit.

She didn't have enough time.

"He's a very dangerous man, Chad." She leaned forward and rested her head in her hands. "I have to go. Watch your back." Charlie hung up the phone.

The commander parked next to the SUV. He turned off the engine and asked, "When everyone finds out what?"

Could she trust Orr with the truth? Or would he hand her over to the government to be poked and prodded? She'd only known him for a few weeks. Had they built any kind of rapport that might work in her favor?

She stared at the warehouse in front of them. Demarco and Allwood were inside. Terrible things could be happening, and only she and Orr could stop it. No one else. If she'd trusted the commander to have her back in this situation, couldn't she trust him with the truth, too?

"We need to find a way inside before it's too late." Charlie unbuckled her seatbelt.

The commander touched her on the arm. "What's going on, Cutter? What dangerous man are you talking about?" He scanned the dark building. "Is there something I need to know before I go in there?"

Charlie let out a measured breath of air. By herself, she was no match for the two men inside. They'd rip each other to pieces. Together, she and Orr could stop them—maybe. "Dr. Stern called me while we were at the hospital lab. She told me the DNA results had come in." Her heart pounded. To say the words aloud made her feel faint. "I was a match."

Orr's brow wrinkled. "A match for what?"

"Armas is my half-brother." She looked down at her hands in her lap. It was hard to believe she'd only received the information herself earlier that day. It felt like a lifetime.

"What?" The commander flinched. "How is that possible?"

With the truth out, she couldn't hold back the rest. "Armas is Bryon Allwood's son. The translations in the text, plus what Angel told me—well, it's the only possible conclusion. Years ago, Allwood arrived in a pod that landed in Corpus Christi. He somehow met my mother and then disappeared before my brother and I were born. My mother thought he had died. He's my father—the man who started this whole thing, who created these time machines, who murdered that poor woman in the hospital, and he seems bent on continuing his dangerous experiments no matter the cost. Now can you see why my brother might be in danger? Why I might be in danger? You think the government would let the two of us lead normal lives knowing we're connected to Allwood?"

Orr sat still and quiet.

"Sir?" His silence unnerved her.

"Is that why you could translate the text so easily?"

"I never knew my real father. I don't know that my abilities had anything to do with—"

Orr tipped his head backward. "Then how did you do it?" He ran a hand down his face. "How?"

"I don't know." She shook her head. "I've always had an ability with languages, codes, puzzles."

He held up a hand. "Stop. I don't have time for this." He worked his jaw. "What you just told me? I can't handle it. Not now." He pointed at the warehouse. "We've got to deal with this shit. The fact you are some time traveler's kid? I don't even know what to do with it. I'm barely keeping up here—the stuff about Demarco? Now this?" He gave a strangled cry. "I don't have a choice right now but to work with you. You understand?"

She nodded.

He pointed a finger in her face. "Don't fucking dare double cross me, Cutter. You got it? I need to know you have my back."

"And I need to know you have mine. That you aren't

going to hand me and my brother over to some agency once this is over."

"You have my word." His back straightened. "I have more questions for you."

"I know."

"Just because I'm not asking them now, doesn't mean I don't want answers later. I barely can grasp the concept of time travel, much less the fact you are a half-sister to a boy who was born five hundred years ago."

"If it helps, I'm still trying to grasp it, too. Everything I thought I knew about myself, my parents, my life—"

"Understood." He stared out at the warehouse. "You ready?"

Charlie nodded.

They both exited the truck and approached the forbidding building.

Were they too late? Demarco had traveled through time to seek out his vengeance on the professor. It was an anger so deeply seated, Charlie feared what they might find inside.

CHAPTER 24

DEMARCO REELED BACK after Allwood told him the content of the email on Kellerman's phone. "That isn't true." His mind went completely blank. "You're lying."

Smart, beautiful Charlie could never be this evil man's daughter.

Never.

Impossible.

Nausea filled his stomach.

"Oh?" The wounded and weakened older man seemed to grow stronger. He scanned Demarco's face. "So you care for this girl?" His thin lips curled up in a wicked smile. "Maybe even love her?"

"Shut up." Suddenly, the room was too small, the air too stale. "Show me the rest. Show me every goddamn thing in this place that you've been doing. I want to see all of it. Come on, get up!" He grabbed Allwood by his broken arm and yanked him out of the chair.

Allwood cried out in pain.

The sound made Demarco happy inside. He wanted

more of it. Every dark thought he'd ever had about Byron Allwood filled his mind.

The older man bent over and hobbled toward the door. "I wonder what Charlene would think of you if she could see you now? Torturing her father and treating him worse than a dog." The smirk had been wiped off his face and replaced with a grimace.

Pain made Allwood obey. Pain made him listen.

"You are not her father." Demarco dragged the man out of the room and pushed him toward the stairs. "Charlie is nothing like you and never will be."

"Charlie, yes, Charlie." Allwood grabbed the railing and slowly took a step down. "So she was able to translate the text, when no one else could. Seems as if my experiment, as you call it, worked as planned."

"Take me to your research," Demarco barked, ignoring the man's remarks. All of his focus needed to be on destroying everything. "Where do you keep your samples? There must be more in this place than one room. Show me or you'll have worse than a broken arm."

"Didn't you wonder how she did it? Why was it so easy for her?"

They reached the bottom of the stairs, and Allwood headed to the left.

"She's a very intelligent woman." Demarco kept his voice cool, but he wanted to scream.

My God, Charlie—his daughter? Why did it have to be him? Why?

"Ah, but she's more than that." The professor hugged his injured arm closer to his body. "The DNA manipulation. The attempts to build a better human—she is proof that it worked. Her intellect must far surpass the norm. Do you know how many centuries were spent trying to translate the Voynich manuscript? Everyone thought it impossible."

As they headed toward a set of double doors at the end of a short corridor, Demarco thought about when he'd first met Charlie—a pretty young woman in Navy summer whites accompanied by Stormy. They'd been about to hop on a plane for North Dakota. He'd thought her too new, too untested for the job, a poor choice for such an assignment. But she'd proven him wrong. Every time he thought she'd break under the pressure, she'd surpassed his expectations.

And now he knew why.

It was as if a cold ocean wave hit him.

Charlie was so accomplished and so capable and so ahead of everyone else because she wasn't a normal human being. She was altered. Had she known she was different? Was it something she could sense?

Nobody else had been able to translate the text, and then this slip of a girl, barely out of college, managed to figure it all out in a few weeks?

His mind jumped to the last time he saw her, crawling out of the overturned SUV, a hurt look on her face as he'd grabbed Allwood and ran. She'd trusted him, and he'd betrayed her for his own purposes. He was so focused on Allwood, he didn't even take a few moments to make sure she was all right. How easy it had been to do it, and he hated himself for it.

He shoved his captive forward, and a rush of delight flowed through him when the older man whimpered.

Charlie, you don't know what kind of man you fell for.

He'd learned to be callous and cruel. Once he'd made the

time jump, he'd had nothing to care about, nothing to live for. All that had mattered was revenge. A seething hate had grown inside him over the years, and he'd tamped it down as best he could and pretended to the new world around him that he was exactly like them. But he knew he wasn't. He knew he'd done horrible things no one in this time would be able to understand.

But, Charlie, you could've changed all of that. If only...

"Charlie is very special," Demarco said quietly. "She's nothing like you."

Allwood reached the doors. These were not protected with a key code. "Once this is over, promise you'll let me go. Promise you'll let me live out my existence in peace."

"What made you think I'd promise you anything?"

The lights snapped on.

A huge space filled with rows and rows of 'rooms' crafted out of thick plastic sheeting appeared before them.

"What is this?" Demarco strode ahead of the limping professor and pulled back the sheeting of the first room he saw. Microscopes, petri dishes, and scientific equipment he didn't recognize covered the top of a stainless steel table on wheels. Small green mini pods sat inside glass boxes on another smaller table—one had partly disintegrated and another seemed to be changing color from green to gray. "Are you still perfecting the formula?"

Allwood sidled up next to him, huffing. Blood loss and pain seemed to be draining the energy from him. He would be so easy to kill, but Demarco had to know everything first. How many people worked in this massive warehouse? Who else had access to the data? He wanted no one to be able to recreate the vile machine that had taken him away from his family, that had separated him from his sister forever, that had brought him nothing but sorrow and loneliness. If he could spare others from such a fate, he would do it. No matter what it took. Since there was no way for him to travel back to Risa, everything would have to end here.

"These are some of our prototypes, yes. You have no idea how long it took me to reach this level of work." Allwood entered the space, his eyes aglow. "Risa had been the true architect of the material we needed. It had been her vision. I only understood it at a basic level. But I've learned so much since then." He picked up the case with the partially disintegrated orb. "The material needs to be flexible, yet strong, living yet capable of resisting forces that would destroy most organic life. Because it is alive, you know."

Demarco crossed to another room hidden behind plastic. "What about other work? Other experiments? This can't be the only thing you're working on here." When he peeled back the sheeting, he saw more pods, more equipment.

"That's everything. I needed another machine. That's all I wanted. These fools in the military were more than happy to give me everything I asked for to create one. I wrote all kinds of proposals for the government, hoping the next one would grab someone's attention. All I needed were a few assistants, some money. I knew they couldn't resist what I was selling—a machine that could travel through time."

"You told them you were from the future?"

"Of course not. That would've been ridiculous." Allwood set the pod on the table and followed Demarco. "But I had enough knowledge to sound as if I knew what I was talking about. You'd be surprised how easy it is to convince a senator or a general to throw a few million dollars your way—especially if you tell them you might sell your work to the highest bidder. When I was awarded my first contract, I left Corpus Christi and Charlie's mother. I didn't need to be saddled with that kind of responsibility."

The emotionless way he spoke of abandoning a woman pregnant with his children disgusted Demarco. Had she merely been a diversion until Allwood achieved what he wanted?

Demarco moved to the next room. It was better to focus on what was in front of him. He couldn't let his emotions get the best of him, or he'd act in haste. He needed to be methodical about what he would do. There was no room for mistakes. When he pushed past the plastic, he saw more green goo, more half-constructed pods. Could it be that Allwood was only interested in traveling to Risa? That all of this time and effort and money—and the death of Kellerman —had only ever been about reuniting with her? The answer seemed too simple.

"You aren't going to stop, are you?" Demarco gestured at the different attempts at creating the correct material. "This warehouse is full of prototypes. That's not the sign of a man who is done with his research."

"I swear to you, I am." Allwood crept toward him and lifted his good arm in the air. "I swear."

Before Demarco could act, the older man brought a heavy glass beaker down on his head.

CHAPTER 25

ORR AND CHARLIE circled the outside of the warehouse looking for signs of life and a way inside. The rusted metal siding covering it screamed for a new coat of paint. Guess the military spent its money on expensive experiments rather than building maintenance. The few visible windows were either covered up or too high to peek through.

The commander, who'd found an old flashlight under a blanket in the cab of the truck, played it across the structure. "I don't see any activity, nor do I see any sign labeling this place a laboratory."

Charlie approached a door on the side of the building and tried opening it. "They have to be in there. Why would Kellerman and Demarco park outside the same warehouse? This has to be Allwood's lab." She made her way around back. "Besides, if you were doing classified research, would you really put a sign up advertising the fact?"

"Point taken," Orr said. As she headed toward the back of the building, he lit up her path. "Be careful. There's a lot of boxes and junk piled around here. I'm surprised the Base Commander doesn't crack down on it. If I were in charge—"

The back of the warehouse was even darker. None of the street lighting reached that far. She stumbled over a rock, nearly losing her balance. But there was another door back here.

"Hey, look, a keypad." This had to be the entry point. The side door didn't have such a lock. She smoothed her fingers over the keys. "We enter through here."

A ripple of fear ran through her. The quietness made her think the worst had already happened. What could they be walking into?

Orr flicked on his flashlight and lit up the keypad. "We don't know the code, and we don't have time to make guesses."

"Give me a minute. We might get lucky." Charlie went into code breaking mode. What number sequence would Allwood use? Maybe she could figure it out. She tried the year of his arrival: 1996. A red light lit up next to the numbered keys.

Nothing.

As she entered different codes, Orr tried the door, then ran his hands along the door jam, as if he could find a secret weakness to exploit. After a few minutes with no result, he grunted. Then he stepped back and examined the whole side of the warehouse.

Charlie was oblivious. She rooted around in her mind, running through the code possibilities. What about the letters on the keypad? Maybe Allwood used a word code instead of a number code.

"Waste of time, Petty Officer." Orr's voice sounded far away.

She waved him off and continued trying codes: numbers, letters, number and letter combos.

Wait, what about the obvious? RISA.

Suddenly, she heard the roar of an engine. The old truck drove up alongside the building, made a big U-turn, and positioned itself behind her. The solid front of the truck faced the wall of the warehouse.

What was he doing?

She turned, and the blast of light from the headlights nearly blinded her. She held up her arm in front of her eyes.

He leaned his head out the window. She could barely make out his silhouette. "Move!" He waved a hand.

The engine revved.

God, he was going to ram it.

Her heart seized. She scrambled away from the keypad, the door, and the building.

No way to sneak up on Allwood and Demarco now.

Once Charlie moved out of the path, the commander let off the brake. The truck barreled toward the rusty warehouse. Repurposed Vietnam War era warehouses might seem indestructible, but both of them were about to find out if that was true.

As the front end of the truck crashed into the door, the wall caved in around it. A godawful screeching coupled with a loud boom echoed into the desert surrounding the base.

CHAPTER 26

BYRON ALLWOOD SMASHED the glass beaker across Demarco's brow.

The bastard.

Pain exploded behind his eyes. Warm, wet blood ran like a stream down his face. Head wounds always were a mess of blood. He touched his forehead.

Shit.

A tiny tremor of fear swept through him.

Allwood had tricked him into believing he was weak and losing strength by the minute. Somehow the old beast was tougher than he'd thought. Maybe a result of his DNA experiments?

Before the special agent could act, the professor followed up his surprise attack with a slash to Demarco's neck using a sliver of broken glass.

Heat seared across his throat. He clutched at the new wound and backed up a few steps into a wall of plastic sheeting.

The older man limped forward, his face a mask of fury.

"You destroyed everything in my old life. I'm not going to let you do it again." He gripped the broken glass so hard, blood dripped from his good hand. "You are too stupid to understand, too pathetic to see what could be. We'll end up right back where we started if nobody tries to change things, tries to make humans better than the animals they are now." He slashed the air.

Demarco pressed up against the sheeting, feeling behind him for an escape route or something he could use as a weapon. Blood dripped steadily into his right eye, blinding him. He wiped at his head wound with the back of his arm. "How would we know what to change in this time, Allwood?" The man believed he could alter the future? What madness was this? "We don't even know when the *Zhadang* happened or if it even happened. Everything we learned as children was built off of long ago memories. We don't know if it's true."

Allwood's eyes snapped in the dim lighting. "We could see the ruin all around us. The shells of buildings and technology that surpassed what I have in this very warehouse. What could I achieve with the better brain I've created, the stronger body, and with Risa by my side—" He let out a strangled cry and lunged at Demarco.

This time, the older man didn't catch him off guard. Demarco bent his head down, let out an animalistic growl, and rushed at Allwood, butting him in the gut. Adrenaline surged through him so, at first, he didn't feel the second slice of the glass across his scalp.

The two tumbled to the ground together. Allwood let out an agonizing yelp when he landed on his broken arm.

Demarco grabbed hold of Allwood's wrist and banged his

hand on the concrete floor, forcing the piece of glass out of his grasp. Then he pressed a knee into the professor's chest using his full weight. He didn't care if Allwood suffocated.

The professor spat in his face. "Not every community did as well as yours. Some of us starved. Some of us watched our friends die, our brothers and sisters, our parents. And nobody cared. Nobody came to make sure we had enough to eat, enough wood to heat our homes. By spring, we were left to raise ourselves...the children who'd made it. Buried our dead who'd been left in the barn all winter, chewed by rats and God know what other creatures." He gasped for air. "Do you know what a body looks like after its been nibbled on for months? What parts do you think a rat likes best? The soft parts—the eyes, the lips, the face. You think I should've left well enough alone? Look around you." With his bloody hand he gestured at the lab. "The technology we have. The ease of living. All the things our families should have had. But no, some stupid idiotic fools hundreds of years before we were born ruined it all. Destroyed everything. With no thought or care about those of us who came after. I'm not going to let that happen again."

"Shut up." Demarco leaned into his face. "I don't want to hear your excuses. Are you trying to make me feel sorry for you? You aren't the only one who suffered loss, who saw horrible things, who walks around every day with memories he tries to forget, tries to put behind him, tries to pretend never happened."

But the man's words did affect him. They dredged up hard winters, summers with too much rain and devastated crops, serious illness and horrible deaths. Things people living in the twenty-first century couldn't even fathom.

"Yet you hate that I wanted to find a way to change that misery? People joined the Genesis Project because they were begging for a better life—begging *me*."

Demarco stared at the older man and blinked. He released a small amount of pressure on Allwood's chest.

Everything he'd thought about Allwood's followers changed in that instant. They were people who'd wanted something better, something more. He'd lumped them into one pile: the enemy. Because they were different than he was. Because they hoped for an escape from the difficult lives they'd led in the aftermath of a long-ago war. As he thought about the wonders around him: electric lights, automatic heating and cooling, even the clothing on his back—the way he'd grown up had been a struggle every day.

Could he blame people for wanting to make a change? Could he blame them for trusting the wrong person?

An explosion of sound broke them apart—a screeching, deafening roar. The walls around them shuddered, and Demarco thought the ceiling high above would collapse on top of them, bury them, and end everything.

He closed his eyes and waited.

———

Charlie's breath caught in her throat. She scanned the devastation left behind in the truck's wake. The wall around the door had bent and then caved as if a boulder had smashed into it. Hard to believe an old pickup could do so much damage. As she stepped through the ruins, twisted metal, pink insulation, and live electric wiring blocked her path.

"Be careful." The commander pushed open the truck's driver's side door, which was blocked by the mangled door frame, and squeezed his body through the opening. "Let me grab the flashlight."

The wiring sparked. She sidestepped it.

A set of stairs led up to a second floor, but debris littered the bottom few steps making passage difficult. Charlie picked her way through it. Spying a broken two-by-four that had once framed the door, she grabbed it. At least she had some kind of weapon. Nothing in Boot Camp had prepped her for this. She knew about gas masks, water tightness, even how to fight a fire on board a ship—but what if she had to engage in hand-to-hand combat? Her legs trembled beneath her.

The commander appeared with the flashlight in one hand and a crowbar in the other. "Come on, we only have a few minutes to take advantage."

"Advantage?"

"I'll bet they weren't expecting a truck to drive through the wall."

Charlie nodded. The upstairs appeared dark, but down the hall a faint glow under a set of double doors caught her attention. "This way, sir!"

They burst through the doors into a massive space full of plastic sheeting creating dozens of individual enclosed spaces.

Where was Angel? Kellerman? Allwood?

The massive impact had knocked over some of the temporary walls, exposing lab equipment, computers, and greenish blobs of all shapes and sizes encased in glass. Some of them had fallen and broken open, a familiar green ooze spilling onto the concrete floors.

Movement caught her eye. Two men grappled on the floor. Angel, blood dripping from a head wound, had his hands around Allwood's throat. The older man's face was turning blue.

She rushed the men and raised her weapon. "Stop it, Angel! Let him go!"

Angel stiffened, looked up, and gave her a hardened glare, a look she'd never seen in his eyes before.

He knew.

He knew she was Allwood's child.

Angel's words resounded in her head: *Any child of Allwood's would be an abomination.*

Although she tightened her grip on the wood, she took a step back. A splinter pressed into her palm.

"Demarco," Orr said, "it's over. Don't make this worse on yourself."

Allwood took advantage of the distraction and the loosened grip around his throat and scrambled away, putting distance between him and his captor.

Angel sat back on his heels and let his arms fall to his sides. "Kellerman's dead."

A wave of shock ripped through her. "My God." She lowered her makeshift weapon. "Did you—?" Her gaze locked with Angel's. She couldn't say the words. Had he lost control? Was Kellerman his first victim and Allwood his next?"

His brow wrinkled. "No, of course not. Do you really think I would? That I'd be capable of—?" He looked down at his hands that had been at Allwood's throat only moments earlier. Color rose in his cheeks. "You don't understand: he attacked me."

"Professor," the commander asked, "are you all right? Do you need medical assistance?"

Allwood had scooted away from Angel until his back had hit a cabinet. "Keep him away from me." He touched his throat. The odd position of one arm indicated a serious break.

"Kellerman died in a pod that lunatic built." Angel pointed at the older man. "He's trying to rebuild the machines. God knows what he planned on doing with them. We have to destroy this place and everything in it."

Charlie looked more closely at the equipment around her, the mini-orbs of green, some still encased in their protective glass, others spilled on the floor.

She picked up an unbroken glass container with a perfect round blob inside it. "Are there more full-size pods?"

Orr, Angel, and Charlie turned to look at Allwood.

Distant sirens sounded.

"They'll be here soon," Allwood said in strained voice. He struggled to his feet. "Who do you think they'll protect?" A cold smile spread across his pale face.

"Why, you son of bitch," Angel growled and stepped forward.

Orr grabbed him by the arm. "We've made enough of a mess as it is." The lights flickered as if to emphasize his statement. He scanned the length of the massive space. "There's a lot of money in this room. The last thing we want to do it piss off the wrong people."

"Sir," Charlie positioned herself between her estranged father and her teammates, "we are the only ones who understand the implications of this kind of research. Think about what might happen if the military could create workable pods."

"But you know what will happen, don't you, Charlie?" Allwood turned his odd eyes on her. "Base security will show up, arrest the three of you, and my work will continue. The commander knows he's in over his head. If you help me complete the formula, I'll say you're my assistant and that these two were the instigators. We could work together— father and daughter."

Orr shifted his focus to Charlie.

"Shut up!" Demarco hissed between clenched teeth. "Leave her out of this." He struggled to pull out of the commander's firm grasp, but his injuries had weakened him.

If Angel hadn't figured out her parentage yet, he knew everything now. She swallowed her fear. "I don't want any part of this. I don't care who you are."

The sirens grew louder.

"They're almost here. Last chance, Charlie. You could continue your work on the translations. Didn't it feel right using that magnificent mind for something so impossible? A challenge where no one else had succeeded? I understand that desire."

"You don't know anything about me. You abandoned my mother and left her to raise me and my brother alone." The chunk of wood rested heavily in her hands. She'd never been a violent person, but Allwood was pushing her to her limits. "You don't care about me. You don't care about my mind. You only care about your obsessive need to be better than human, to be smarter than everyone else."

A laugh sputtered from his thin lips. "I understand you

well enough to know you want to use your intelligence. You crave finding a puzzle worth solving, a mystery worth uncovering. Real work. Real achievement. Real discovery. I made you that way, Charlie. I created you, whether or like it or not."

"Stop it. You didn't make me." But deep inside she had doubts. Deep inside she worried about what ran through her bloodstream. Was she normal? Was she a freak? Is that why she felt as if she never fit in? Too smart, too fast, too everything. The only one who'd understood had been her brother. He hadn't struggled with the differences as much as she.

"You bastard," Angel spat out. "Let me throttle him." He managed to break free of Orr's grip and lunged at the professor.

"Demarco, stop!" Orr commanded and raised the crowbar he held.

The special agent tackled Allwood, and they landed in a heap.

The faint smell of smoke hovered in the air.

The electrical wiring that sparked earlier must have set off a blaze.

"Shit. A fire will rip through this place," Orr said. "We don't have much time."

The two injured men grappled on the floor.

"Angel, please!" Charlie held the two-by-four in her hands. She didn't want to hurt anyone, but if she had to, she would. "We have to go."

Orr dropped the crowbar, grabbed Allwood by his good arm, and hauled him up and away from Demarco. "This ends now. The fire will be our cover."

The smoke grew thicker.

"What about Allwood?" The special agent, disheveled and bloody, spat on the floor. "He murdered someone. We can't let him get away with it—and we can't let the experiments here continue."

"Agreed." Orr's gaze flicked from Demarco to Allwood. "Security will be here any minute. What do you suggest we do?"

The lights flickered out and plunged the warehouse into darkness.

CHAPTER 27

A FEW DIM emergency lights kicked on.

Orr snapped on his flashlight and bounced the thin beam of light off the plastic sheeting around them.

"I think we take him with us," Charlie said, "and hope the fire destroys everything. Without Allwood or Kellerman, that should slow down their research."

"Slow it down?" Angel's nostrils flared. "No, it has to end." With a grunt, he swept his arm across a stainless steel table covered in organic samples and knocked them all to the floor. Shards of glass and goo flew in all directions. Then he ripped through the next plastic partition like a bull through a matador's cape and dumped over another table. "I won't have them hurting anyone else." He shoved a chair out of his way and proceeded to the next space.

"He's lost his mind," said the professor as Orr made sure he stayed put.

Charlie chased after him. "Angel, wait!"

"Kellerman died in one of those machines. He'll convince

someone else it's safe, toss them in a pod, watch them die. How many times is he allowed to do that before someone stops him? What about the possibility of using the pods? What would the military change if they got the chance? That sort of power is too dangerous."

"What happened to Kellerman was horrible." Charlie shivered at the image that popped into her mind. He didn't deserve that. "But if we're caught here, we'll end up in prison. What we've seen tonight must be protected behind a slew of special access requirements. They'll never let us out or we might reveal their secrets."

Angel's eyebrows came together. "At least Kellerman managed to erase any trace of their work from the computer systems."

"What?"

"Kellerman might be a traitor, but he managed to set off some sort of automated self-destruct. Allwood tried to stop it, but I don't think he succeeded. They should be operating on an intranet like we do back at the office, right?"

Charlie nodded. Even though Angel hated tech, he'd learned a few things at least. "So no data storage outside of this building." She scanned the dimly lit space around them. "The only bits of formula they have left are the samples in this room?"

"Right." Angel breathed heavily and wiped at the blood still dripping down his forehead.

"Hey, I have an idea." Orr played his flashlight across the wall next to another exit door blocked with some high shelves covered in cardboard boxes.

"What is it?" Charlie eyed Angel. Would he be able to

contain his rage and wait until they could make a coherent plan? "Security will be here any minute." She coughed.

The smoke grew thicker.

The commander had forced the professor to walk to the wall he'd lit up. "It's a deluge system. Not very common, but makes sense in a space this size."

"Deluge system?" Charlie asked.

"The sprinklers above us. Instead of a fire sprinkler being set off individually due to heat, a deluge system releases water all at once from every sprinkler simultaneously." He tapped a fire alarm next to a complex system of pipes. "Only have to pull this."

"But that will put out the fire," Angel said. "We want this place to burn."

"With this kind of system, there's no way the place will burn down. Eventually, the conditions in the building will set it off automatically," Orr pointed out. "But the problem isn't the building, it's the organic materials they're trying to recreate."

"Yes." Angel's body straightened.

"The organic materials dissolve in water." Charlie picked up on the commander's thinking. They'd seen it several times already—a pod landed in the water and then liquefied into nothing within minutes. "I think you have something there, sir."

"Without the computer data, plus making sure we dissolve all the samples—it would make it impossible for research to go forward. Especially with Allwood gone."

"Gone?" The professor jerked his head. "Where am I going?"

"You're coming with us to Nellis," explained Orr. "We have an extra seat for you on the flight back to DC."

"You can't do that to me." The older man attempted to wrench free of Orr's grasp. "I'll call the senator. She'll put a stop to this."

"Who said you get a phone call?" Angel gave a wicked smile barely visible in the low light.

The sirens grew even closer.

"Sir, we have to work fast before it's too late." Charlie lifted her head to look across the rows of temporary walls. Could they finish in time?

"I'll take care of this one first," Orr lifted slightly on the professors twisted arm. "You two start smashing and dumping."

Angel and Charlie looked at each other. He gave her a wavering smile. For now they trusted each other. But after it was all over? What would he do to the daughter of his enemy?

A chill ran through her.

Angel and Charlie each selected a row of cells to tackle and methodically smashed beakers and containers in each one. Any green goo had to be exposed. Mini refrigerators were overturned and contents spilled onto the concrete floor.

Charlie used her chunk of wood to sweep across counters and tables. Using brute force, Angel overturned everything in sight. The floor was awash with broken glass and clumps of the experimental pod material.

The smoke in the space grew thicker. The sprinklers would go off any moment.

Orr quickly secured Allwood with an extension cord and muzzled him with some duct tape, then grabbed a large garbage can at the end of one of the rows. "Put any slides in here. A can full of water should ruin them."

Charlie scooped up two trays of glass slides sitting next to a microscope and discarded them into the container. Angel passed her with a stack of trays to do the same.

Orr dragged the can to the middle of the space and joined them in tearing the place apart.

The sirens intensified.

"Faster," the commander said. "We don't have much time."

The three of them scrambled.

Angel threw more trays of slides into the can. "Done."

The build-up of smoke finally set off the deluge system. No need to pull the alarm. Every sprinkler head in the massive warehouse turned on simultaneously. Sheets of water poured into the space.

Charlie jumped when the cold water hit her skin and dropped the two-by-four. She still had several trays full of samples to expose. "Angel, help me."

The special agent rushed to her aid and burst through the sheeting behind her to reach the last of the organic samples and mini-pods.

Through the high windows, red flashing lights bounced off the ceiling.

"They're here." Orr trotted toward their captive. "We have to leave. Now."

"Give me a second." Angel kicked over the last refrigerator, and the remaining samples spilled out. Water from the sprinklers melted the experimental substance into a greenish watery mess, which drained into a grate near the center of the space.

"It's working." Charlie swept an arm across her brow to clear her vision and watch as the organic materials turned into liquid.

"This way!" Orr held Allwood by the cord that entrapped him. He headed in the direction of an emergency exit on the side of the building.

Charlie and Angel stared at one another. The force of the water rained down on them.

"Are you coming with us?" she asked. Would he want to be part of their team, or would he balk at associating with Allwood's daughter?

His face was unreadable. Her mind flicked back to his attitude in Devils Lake—although he'd been part of NCIS-A, he'd been operating alone and with his own agenda. No wonder he'd kept to himself and had a standoffish demeanor. Now she and Orr had showed up at the lab and had ruined his plans.

"Let's go." Angel grabbed her by the elbow and helped her across the slick concrete floors toward the exit through which Orr had already disappeared.

His touch on her arm was comforting. She wanted to believe he'd changed and that he understood her connection to Allwood was not her fault. But maybe this sudden decision to work with her and Orr was merely about his own escape, his own survival.

They burst through the exit doors.

Charlie shivered in the cool desert air, her wet clothes clammy against her skin.

The emergency vehicles had pulled around back where the smoke and flames had probably been most visible. They only had mere moments to act before they'd be discovered.

"Your keys," the commander held out a hand. "Give them to me."

Angel lifted his chin. "If I can be in charge of Allwood."

Orr scanned the professor. His shoulders were rounded, his head hung low. "Fine. He shouldn't be much trouble now."

Angel handed Orr the keys to the stolen SUV, and the commander shoved the professor in his direction.

They crept around to the front of the warehouse. A murmur of voices drifted toward them from the crash site at the back. More help might show up any minute.

Orr pressed a button and unlocked the vehicle. Angel shoved Allwood into the back seat, quietly shut the door, and then opened the hatchback.

Charlie's brow wrinkled.

The commander was more interested in leaving the scene without being noticed, rather than paying attention to Angel.

The special agent closed the hatchback and handed Charlie a plaid picnic blanket. "You look cold. Maybe this will help."

She accepted the blanket without a word. Angel climbed into the back with the professor. As she took the front passenger seat, she wrapped the musty-smelling fabric around her shoulders. Maybe he didn't hate her after all?

Orr started the car, backed out slowly, and drove away

from the warehouse without any headlights. As they neared the base entrance, the commander turned them on, but also made a phone call. "We'll be ready for wheels up in three hours," he said to someone on the other end.

The guard who'd let them onto base must've recognized the SUV as Allwood's because he opened the gate before they even arrived.

As the gate shut behind them, Orr, Demarco, Charlie, and Allwood sped for the highway.

CHAPTER 28

AS THEIR PLANE took off from Nellis Air Force Base, Charlie stared at the seat Kellerman had occupied when they'd arrived. Although she knew he was dead, she had trouble processing it. She'd spent many long hours working with him, talking to him, getting to know him. It would be difficult knowing his family would never hear the true story of his death. How horrible.

Commander Orr approached her holding two steaming Styrofoam cups. "You look as if you could use a warm drink."

She accepted the coffee, and the picnic blanket slipped off one shoulder. "Thank you."

Orr shifted his gaze to the back of the plane where the special agent, his wounds now bandaged, sat next to the restrained professor. "I'm not sure I can trust him with Allwood, but what choice do I have? It's a long flight back to Andrews. We need an eye on that guy until we decide what to do with him."

"What are we going to do? With his lab destroyed, he's

the only one with any information about how to create more machines. People are going to start looking for him."

"I know." He sipped his coffee. "But until we read the reporting on the fire at the lab, we have to keep our heads down."

"The guards know we were there. Won't someone start asking questions?"

"Let me worry about that, Cutter." Orr's friendly, relaxed demeanor shifted into serious commanding officer mode. "I don't know about you, but it's been a long and confusing day."

Her gut clenched. In the lab, she'd spilled the truth about her background. Now both Angel and Orr knew everything. What would happen to her?

"Don't worry, Petty Officer." It was as if the commander read her mind. "Your secret is safe with me. You and your brother will have nothing to worry about."

"But the DNA—"

"I'll take care of it," he said.

"I don't understand how that's possible."

"Dr. Stern has a very good relationship with the head of the lab at NSA. They're used to providing classified results to a host of federal customers." He tapped a finger on the side of his cup. "Besides, they don't really know why we were processing these samples. At this point, we can ask for them to be destroyed."

"True." If the DNA results went no further than the NCIS-A office, shouldn't that be the end of it? "But Demarco—"

She looked over her shoulder. Angel's penetrating gaze met hers. She shivered and turned around.

"I'll speak to him."

Did the commander understand the pure hatred Angel felt, not only for Allwood, but for all of his followers? Even his own sister? She didn't trust him. He could decide to turn on her at any moment to rid himself and the world of an 'abomination.' What about Chad? Would he ever be safe from Angel's wrath?

"I don't know if that will be enough." Orr was seriously underestimating the depths of Angel's feelings. She'd seen them first-hand. The fire in his eye when he spoke of members of the Genesis Project altering their DNA still shook her to her core.

"Drink your coffee, get some sleep, and we can all talk about this tomorrow at the office." Orr patted her arm.

When he moved to rise from his seat, she grabbed his sleeve. "Don't leave me alone."

His brow wrinkled. "Today really shook you up, huh?"

"Why don't you look at me differently after finding out I'm Allwood's daughter?"

"Why should that matter to me?" He angled his body to face her. "It did shock me to hear it, and it took a little bit of brain power to understand how that was possible, but the minute I began believing in time traveling pods, it wasn't too hard to come around to it." He shrugged. "If your connection to Allwood is what helped you translate the manuscript, I'm glad you're here working for the good guys."

She nodded. "I don't want anyone on the team to look at me differently or treat me differently. Nothing has changed. I'm still Charlene Cutter."

"That's exactly who I still need on this team. You're an excellent asset to the group. I'd be crazy to let you go."

"Thank you, sir." A sudden lightness filled her. "I don't want to work anywhere else."

Orr flashed a smile. "Good."

CHAPTER 29

DEMARCO WATCHED as Orr and Charlie chatted. Inside he was a writhing mass of conflicting emotions. After today, where did he belong? He'd reached his years-long goal: finding the man who'd stolen his sister and destroyed his life. Now what?

The knowledge to build the machines no longer existed except in the pages of a manuscript only Charlie seemed able to translate and the mind of the man seated next to him. Demarco was stuck. A man between lives, between times. A stranger here, yet not a stranger. He'd never return home, and he'd never travel to his sister. He wiped the grit from his eyes. Any trust he'd built with the team had been irrevocably destroyed by his actions. What would happen to him once they landed?

"I'm thirsty," Allwood said.

The older man didn't look good—broken, bleeding, weak. It was as if the battle they'd fought in the warehouse had used up the last of his energy.

"I suppose I could give you some water." Demarco tested

the plastic restraints the commander had used once they'd made it to the plane. They seemed solid enough. Besides, where could the man go? They were flying tens of thousands of feet in the air.

He rose from his seat and worked his way forward to grab a bottle of water. As he neared the row where Charlie sat, he felt her eyes on him. It pained him to think about her connection to Allwood. How could such a terrible man produce such an exceptional daughter? Everything he'd told her about how he viewed the followers of the Genesis Project and his feelings toward Armas came to the surface. He fisted his hands. She must hate him.

He grabbed two bottles and headed toward the back of the plane, keeping his gaze unfocused. His work with A Group was probably over. He'd never have to see her again after today. That might make things easier. He could forget. He could go back to the life he'd lived before she came, before he'd managed to lie his way into a job. The lonely, distant life of a man without a past or a future.

When he reached Allwood, he held out the bottle. "Here."

The professor sat slumped in his seat.

Demarco frowned. "Wake up." He prodded the man's good arm with the cold water bottle.

Nothing.

Was he breathing?

"Shit." He grabbed a wrist and felt for a pulse. "Sir, I think we have a medical emergency here."

The thought of losing the one person besides himself who cared about and remembered Risa, hit him hard. Even though Allwood was a murderer, a mad scientist, and a charismatic liar who harmed people and ruined lives, it perturbed him to think he'd no longer exist. Maybe he wanted justice, maybe he wanted vengeance, or maybe something else entirely. But watching Allwood slip away didn't seem fair.

He dragged the man to the floor and began chest compressions.

The professor's eyes were partially open. Demarco shivered at the emptiness in them.

Orr appeared at his side. He didn't know if Charlie was there, too, but what did it matter?

"What did you do?" the commander asked.

"Nothing. I swear to you." He continued to press against the thin man's chest. "He asked for some water, and then when I came back—"

Charlie knelt next to Allwood and picked up a limp wrist. "He doesn't have a pulse."

As Demarco looked down at the man he'd hated, his vision blurred and a heaviness settled in him. "No." Who would he talk to about Risa? Who would understand what it felt like to be transported to a time with nothing and no one familiar?

"He's dead, Angel." Charlie touched his shoulder. "It's too late."

"No." He slowed his rhythmic movements, knowing what she said was true, but not wanting it to be real. "He can't die." He needed this man. He needed someone to hate, someone to blame. Someone who understood.

"It's over."

His shoulders slumped.

"There's nothing else we can do," the commander said.

Demarco grabbed his unopened bottle, grunted, and hurled it at the bulkhead. It exploded in a shower of water.

———

The last few hours of the trip had gone by in silence. Charlie had assumed Angel would be pleased with Allwood's death. But his violent reaction when he threw the water bottle had surprised her. After that, Angel seemed distracted and isolated himself in the last row of seats. The commander had put himself in charge of the body, wrapping it in a tarp that he'd found stowed in one of the cargo nets and dragging it out of the aisle to lay next to the body bag of his follower. Charlie had returned to her precious manuscript translations because it was easier to lose herself in the mysterious symbols rather than assess her feelings about what had happened.

Maybe she was numb to it. Maybe too much had happened too quickly, and now she was in shock. It was hard to know. Byron Allwood was her father, and both he and Kellerman were dead. That was more than enough to jolt the system.

That fact hit her hard: the man she'd always thought of as her father was not.

She reassessed her relationship with Harrison Cutter—the man who had given her her name. He'd taken on a woman pregnant with another man's children, which gave Charlie an entirely different perspective on him. The clashes she'd had with him over the years seemed clearer to her now —the two of them were different, and he knew it. He knew there was no DNA connecting him to her or to Chad.

Anything a parent might be proud of would be seen through that lens. Someone else's child. Someone else's blood. Someone else's joy. Not his.

No wonder her mother had been so defensive of her father's actions over the years. "But he loves you, Charlie," she would always say. "He only wants what's best for you." At the time it had come across as so typical 'dad,' to be over-protective and controlling to the point of irritation. But maybe he had been so protective because he knew the truth. And that truth would've been so damaging and hurtful once it was revealed—their real father had left them, hadn't wanted them, had actually hid himself away for more than twenty years to avoid his responsibilities. Her real father had been a selfish man who didn't care anything about the woman he'd hurt and left pregnant and alone.

What might have been if Byron Allwood would've lived? Her mind was empty of thought. She couldn't think of any situation where she'd insert Allwood into her life. In fact, every scenario she came up with, Harrison Cutter's face filled in. Because he'd been there her whole life. Yes, he drove her crazy. Yes, he could be overbearing and tough. Yes, he expected too much from her. But that was probably because he knew she had the talent to achieve more than she'd dreamed for herself.

What did it matter if the dead man in the plane had given her half her DNA? It meant nothing to her, really. She was Charlie Cutter, and she worked for NCIS-A. None of her achievements were Allwood's. Everything she'd accomplished, she'd done on her own with the support of Harrison Cutter.

Allwood was gone, his work destroyed, and he would

never hurt anyone again—especially not her or her brother. No one beyond her team and her family would ever know the truth about her connection to Allwood. The commander had made clear it changed nothing about how he viewed her or her skills.

She focused on the iPad. The Voynich manuscript symbols leapt off the page at her. She'd found her true calling with her team. How satisfying it had been to feel supported, listened to, and respected, to know that her knowledge, skills, and interests were of value and had purpose.

The plane landed with a thud. They were home.

What would the next assignment be for A Group? Their main directive to pursue any evidence of alien life on earth had been turned upside down when they'd uncovered a time traveling secret that had lain hidden for centuries. Her body tingled at the achievement. But she needed something more. Something equally challenging, equally intriguing. Her mind craved the stimulation.

The commander strolled up to her seat. "So, Petty Officer Cutter, are you looking forward to being back in the office?" The awkward silence that had hung over the last few hours disappeared.

"Actually, I was thinking about Armas." Her half-brother needed her more than ever. "I'd like to visit him, if that's possible."

"We'll have to ask Dr. Stern. He's still very touch-and-go as I understand."

Charlie nodded. She wanted to stay positive about his recovery. He'd been through so much in his short life. "Then it will be good if I stay busy. I hope you have some new work for me." She said it in more of a teasing tone than anything.

They'd have weeks of reports to catch up on regarding what happened in Lake Havasu, and it was still to be discussed if they'd report on what really happened in the warehouse.

"I might have something new up my sleeve," the commander answered mysteriously. "But I'd like to wait for Chief to make it back. The hospital left a message, and he's going to be released later today."

The plane taxied to a stop.

What did Commander Orr have in mind?

———

The small team stood together on the tarmac at Andrews Air Force Base. It was right before dawn, but the rising sun was hidden behind a morass of gray clouds. Only a muted glow told them it was sunrise.

"Dr. Stern is going to meet me here with a transport for the bodies. She'll do some tests and then we'll dispose of them," Orr said. "Word out of Area 51 this morning is that there was a lab accident that caused two deaths. Not sure if they'll bother digging to find out its only Kellerman's remains in the warehouse. Demarco, you said the body was quite damaged."

Angel nodded.

Orr acknowledged his affirmation with a sigh. "There's also a bit of frantic chatter in the intel community about a highly classified project having to be shuttered for the time being."

"Still hard to believe we were able to leave the scene without incident." Charlie thought about how easy it was to drive off into the desert while emergency services worked to stop what was left of the fire. "Are you sure they won't come looking for us?"

Even though Charlie had thought Angel had slept most of the flight home, the dark circles under his eyes told a different story. Would Orr be recommending him for disciplinary measures?

"My base access was tied to another Area 51 office, and the Commanding Officer at NSA Washington approved my request." Orr stood with legs apart and arms crossed. "If they want to take it up with Captain Schultz, they are more than welcome."

"So the truth remains safe behind TOP SECRET YARDARM privileged access only?" Charlie asked.

"Correct. The three of us will combine the details of last night into a report for cleared personnel only, which is quite a small circle," Orr said. "I'll give you two a few days to type something up, then I'll handle the final report."

"Will I still have access to the office?" Angel frowned.

Orr had to know what he was asking: was he in any trouble?

"Of course. You are a necessary part of our team. Especially now that we're down a man. Until we can find a replacement for Kellerman, I'm relying on everyone more than ever."

Angel nodded.

Charlie's stomach twisted. She had a small hope that Angel would be shuttled to a different office after his behavior, so she wouldn't have to see him again. It would be so much easier than having to worry about watching her back. What if Angel turned on her?

Orr changed the subject, "On that note, can you give Petty Officer Cutter a ride back to her room?"

She broke out in a cold sweat.

"Of course, sir." Angel wouldn't look at her.

Charlie opened her mouth to argue, then stopped. What good would it do?

"We'll have a team meeting tomorrow in the office," Orr said. "0730 sharp."

"Yes, sir," she said. Would Orr share everything with the team? Even the most secret of truths?

When the commander headed back up the ramp into the plane, the two of them stared at each other for a few moments. Orr wouldn't send her off with Angel if he thought she would be in danger, would he?

"I'm parked in this direction." Angel pointed using his hand as a directional arrow.

As she followed behind him, her mind was a whirlwind of questions, worries, fears. "Why?" It was the one question that stuck in her mind. "Why did you do it, Angel?"

"I had to." He kept walking with his gaze focused straight in front of him. "Allwood was the only thing that kept me going in this time for many years. Without that motivation, I wouldn't have survived, Charlie."

He spoke her name with a gentleness that surprised her.

She mulled over his answer and willed her heart to slow down.

They reached his Landcruiser, and he unlocked the passenger's side first, opening the door for her. Her stomach fluttered. Why was he being so kind? He hated her father and by extension should hate her.

When he joined her inside the vehicle, he didn't start the engine right away.

Charlie took the opportunity to press him. "Why didn't you explain your fears to Commander Orr? Why did you feel the need to strike out on your own, steal someone's car, take Allwood hostage—"

"And abandon you." Angel gripped the steering wheel. "I'm sorry I left you after the accident, Charlie. I wasn't in my right mind. I had to stop him. Orr would've made me follow the rules, call the authorities, agree to whatever BS the military would do to cover up what they'd been working on. I couldn't let that happen. I couldn't let Allwood get away with it. He was evil, Charlie."

The tiny hairs lifted on the back of her neck. "Which means you think I'm evil, too."

"What?" His posture became rigid.

"I'm his daughter. You must hate me." Her hands shook. She clasped them in her lap so he wouldn't notice.

"Before I met you, I never would've thought this world held anything I'd value. I thought I'd lost everything that mattered. But you proved me wrong, Charlie. There was something in this world that I cherish more than anything else." He turned in her direction, and his eyes searched hers. "Why did you think—?"

Using all the courage she could muster, she met his dark gaze. "I'm tainted, I'm an abomination." But a tiny little piece of her wanted to believe him.

"I was wrong." Tentatively, he touched her arm. "Everything I said was wrong. I understand that now."

"How can I believe you?" She thought back to the moment she'd seen past his rigid exterior and saw the hurt man behind it. Had that ever been real? Who was Angel Demarco? "Am I supposed to forget what you told me?"

"The information we uncovered yesterday exposed Allwood's true feelings toward his followers. My God, he even killed one of them. Those poor people were charmed by that charlatan. He experimented on them as a means of further refining his techniques before he tried the genetic manipulation on himself. It was always about how his followers could benefit him. Even my sister—he used her for her knowledge of plants and organic chemistry to build the time traveling machines. He never intended to take these people with him. I think he merely used them to disappear— one time traveling pod stands out. But a whole host of them landing at once? It was a good cover for someone who never wanted to be found again. It was wrong of me to blame his victims for what he did to them. You were one of them. But what's even worse is you had no choice in the matter." He cupped her cheek in his hand.

Her eyes filled with tears. "And my brother? And Armas? What about them?"

"All I know, is that I can't imagine life without you. I love you, Charlie."

Her pulse raced as he leaned in.

"And if loving you means I have to let go of some of my beliefs and acknowledge some of my wrongheaded thinking, then that's what I have to do." He brushed a strand of hair from her eyes. "I can't go back to the life I had before. I need you."

CHAPTER 30

TWENTY-FOUR HOURS LATER, Charlie, Angel, Stormy, Dr. Stern, and Chief Ricard sat around the conference table in their office, while Commander Orr stood behind the podium. A strange current ran through the room with the notable absence of Kellerman. As each one entered and sat in their usual seats—Kellerman's spot remained empty. Yes, he'd been part of their team, but once Orr explained to everyone what happened on their trip out West and how he'd died, the odd sensation dissipated some. They hadn't really known Kellerman as well as they'd thought.

"I gathered us here this morning to discuss my plans for NCIS-A going forward. I will need each of your expertise to bring this plan to fruition. I presented my idea to the Commanding Officer for NSA Washington, and he signed off on it late yesterday. He was briefed on our mission, and is in full support of this next phase."

"Next phase?" Charlie asked.

Those seated around the table gave each other confused looks.

"Stormy, can you turn off the lights, please?"

The lights dimmed, and the commander projected a slide on the screen. "As we learned on the flight to Nellis, Chief and Kellerman were able to identify dozens of radar signals over the last twenty-five years or so that indicate a pod landing." A world map appeared with a number of different colored dots sprinkled across it. "The yellow dots you see are recent radar signatures captured in the last five years. The red, blue, and green dots are all from older time periods as you can see here." He used a laser pointer to draw attention to a key in the bottom right-hand corner that lined up the different colored dots with different years, going all the way back to 1996—Allwood's arrival.

He clicked to the next slide. "The first part of our initiative will be tracking down these pod landings. We will start from the most recent and work our way backward. The goal will be to find out if there are any survivors. Just like Byron Allwood, Armas, and the woman in the hospital at Lake Havasu, not all pod landings result in the traveler's death. Stormy and Chief will team up on this task. Chief has been studying these signatures for a while now, so he is the most familiar with the locations and the possibility for survival. Petty Officer Storm has a knack for data tracking and, let's face it, she has a kind face. I think witnesses will trust her more easily than some of the rest of us."

Charlie smiled to herself, thinking about the first day she met Angel and what she thought of him.

"What's the second part of our initiative?" Angel asked.

He'd shared with Charlie his nervousness about the meeting. He didn't believe yet that the commander had fully forgiven him for some of his actions in Nevada. In fact, he still expected to lose his clearance and his job, and maybe even face charges.

"I'm glad you asked, Demarco. This second part wouldn't work without you." Orr clicked to another slide that read: *Greeting Committee.*

"What does that mean?" Charlie asked.

"We are expecting more arrivals. We aren't sure how many pods were created—I'm hoping we can use the data in Byron Allwood's phone, recovered by Petty Officer Cutter, to find out more—but because we had three pods land in the last month, more could arrive any day. We need to welcome these people, provide for them, explain where they are and what has happened. Rather than our original mission of hunting down aliens, we are searching for humans who have been lost to time. This will be a humanitarian mission. I'd like Petty Officer Cutter and Special Agent Demarco to head the committee."

"Why did you say the second initiative wouldn't work without Demarco?" Chief asked.

Everyone turned their attention to Angel.

"I don't mean to put you on the spot, Demarco," Orr said, "but the fact is we need your help on this one. I think you should let the rest of the team know why."

Angel blanched.

Charlie hadn't been expecting that. Angel's secret could wreak havoc with the small amount of trust that remained between the team after Kellerman's betrayal.

Orr gave a quick nod. "It's okay, Demarco. They need to know. It will help them understand."

Chief Ricard focused a penetrating gaze at Demarco. He'd already learned the truth about the special agent in

Lake Havasu and had been standoffish ever since he'd entered the conference room. Demarco had, after all, flipped the car that had caused him major injuries. Charlie wasn't sure how the chief truly felt about Angel after finding that out.

"What is it?" asked Stormy. "Why is everyone so quiet?"

Dr. Stern appeared thoughtful.

"It's okay." Charlie laid a hand on Angel's thigh. If he wanted to leave his past behind and accept this new life in a new time, he needed to know when to trust and share his connection to all of this.

Angel looked down at the table and rubbed his hands together. "I don't think I can be a part of this, sir."

The special agent avoided eye contact with everyone in the conference room. "I think it's a mistake for me to continue here. I appreciate the offer, Commander, but I don't think it would work out." He stood, slipped his lanyard and badge over his head, and set it on the table.

Dr. Stern frowned and reached a hand toward him as if she wanted to stop him.

Charlie's brow wrinkled. "Wait, Angel. We can take it slow." She looked to Orr. "Can't we, sir?"

Angel set his jaw. "Please don't, Charlie." He headed for the door. "I'll clean out my desk and go."

As he exited, Charlie scooted back in her chair and shot a glare at her superior. "You're asking too much of him."

Orr raised an eyebrow. "I gave him a pass on everything. I kept the authorities off his back. He owes this office an explanation, and it starts with the truth."

Chief Ricard's lips pressed flat.

Dr. Stern scanned the middle-aged enlisted man who sat across from her. "Don't even think it, Chief."

He held up his hands, palms out. "I didn't say a thing."

"You were thinking it," the doctor said. "You think you're so perfect?"

His mouth gaped open, then closed.

"What's going on?" Stormy asked. "I feel as if I need the CliffNotes." She looked to Dr. Stern.

"Isn't anyone going to stop him?" Charlie looked around the room at what remained of their team. "He might've made some mistakes, but he saved all of us. He stopped a madman from following through on his insane plans."

"Go after him, Charlie," said Dr. Stern.

She nodded and disappeared out the door.

CHAPTER 31

CHARLIE ROUNDED the end of the cubicles and headed straight for Angel's desk. "What do you think you're doing?"

He leaned over a banker's box he had already filled with his jacket and the few sparse personal belongings he'd allowed himself in the office: a single small African violet, a postcard of the Lincoln Memorial, and a visitor's guide to Washington D.C. "I'm cleaning out my desk. What does it look like I'm doing?"

"Everyone wants you to stay on the team."

"I'm not interested."

"Why? Is it because Orr wants you to tell everyone where you came from? Who you are?"

He straightened, leaned against his desk, and rubbed the back of his neck. "That's some of it. Look, I'm packed. I'm going. You can follow me if you want, but I'm not going to change my mind." He picked up his box and headed for the door.

Charlie followed. "What else is there to be afraid of? Everyone back in the conference room is ready to continue forward on our new mission, and once you explain your past, they'll understand why you did what you did. They'll forgive you."

They exited into the hall, which was quiet and empty of foot traffic.

He smirked and shook his head. "Right. They'll forgive me. Even Chief?"

She checked the hall in both directions. "They believe in time travelers now," she whispered. "That would've been the biggest hurdle to overcome."

A pair of men in fatigues walked purposefully toward them.

Charlie and Angel split apart to let them pass.

They both watched the men until they turned a corner and disappeared.

"It's not only the team I'm thinking about." Angel headed toward the elevator in the opposite direction. "I'm more than a time traveler, Charlie. There are things I've done. Things I'm not proud of."

"Haven't we all?" Why was he so scared to own up to his past? This was his 'get out of jail free' moment, and he was squandering it by worrying about how he'd be perceived. Who cared what any of them would think?

He stopped mid-stride. "You don't get it. It's not about telling the team about who I am, it's about things I've done. Things that would terrify you. You'd barely be able to look at me if you knew. Imagine if one of Allwood's followers steps out of a pod and sees me. What if they know who I am? Remember. Orr doesn't understand that, and you barely understand that." He pressed hard on the elevator call button.

"We'll greet them as a team. Show them things can be different in this time. We don't have to be enemies. This is your opportunity."

"And if they don't believe me?" He passed by her to enter the empty elevator.

She followed.

"They will learn to believe, Angel." She touched him on the arm. "I promise. I know you're a good man inside."

His eyes searched her face. "I'm only good when I'm with you."

The elevator doors closed, leaving them alone in the quiet. Only a few floors, and they'd reach their destination.

She met his gaze. "Then don't leave me. Because you are the one that helped me find my true calling, the reason I was born. I'm part of the future but also part of the past." A fluttery feeling intensified in her chest. "We can bridge the divide together."

CHAPTER 32

Six months later....

ANGEL DROVE his Landcruiser down a familiar road in Colchester, Virginia toward the Occoquan River. It was barely past dawn in late February, and a thin veneer of snow lay across everything. The Mid-Atlantic was headed for spring, so this would likely be one of the last snows of the season.

"Looks a lot different in the winter, doesn't it?" Charlie stared out the windshield and wished she'd dressed a little warmer, but she and Angel had been in bed at her new apartment when the alert came through—another pod landing at very familiar coordinates. No time to second-guess her outfit. A local landing was a godsend. She should be glad they didn't have to hop on a plane and fly to Portugal.

"Are you sure these are the right coordinates?" Angel asked.

"Yes." She showed him the yellow dot on her cell phone

from the map Commander Orr had texted her. "You've asked me that three times already."

"It doesn't make any sense."

"Why? Chief showed us the map of all the landings they've tracked from the radar data. About sixty percent of them seem to be clustered around the Maryland-DC-Virginia area for some unknown reason. It makes sense we'd have another landing here."

Angel slowed down as Bell Avenue narrowed, and the woods closed in on them. It would open up soon to reveal the large mansion at the end of the road. The spot where they'd recovered Armas.

Charlie's heart twinged.

Armas.

Her half-brother.

It had taken weeks for him to come out of his drug-induced coma, but ultimately the anti-toxin treatment had worked. He still suffered from some muscle weakness, but Stormy made sure he consistently met with his physical therapist. After he'd been released from the hospital, Stormy had decided she and her husband would become his foster parents—there could be no official adoption, as he had no record of birth and no parents to sign away their rights. A special department that was assisting with their 'Welcome Committee' duties at the Social Security office, helped create documentation that would pass scrutiny once Armas became an adult.

Although Charlie felt a deep attachment to the boy, Stormy had the necessary family structure and support such a child would need to grow up and mature. Stormy's children had bonded with Italian-speaking Armas and had even begun to learn simple Italian phrases using a language learning app. Charlie's life and schedule would've been too erratic to take on such responsibilities, but she and Angel visited him whenever they could. The most shocking thing had been seeing Angel leap into the role of uncle full throttle. His love for his nephew grew each time they visited the Storm house. As time had passed, Armas had begun turning into a regular American boy—so little of his previous life existed in him except for an occasional Italian word or phrase. He was young and adaptable and happy—despite the horrors of his illness and the loss of his mother.

Angel parked the vehicle. "The radar tracking indicated the pod should be landing any minute. Any suggestions for recovery?"

They both stared out at the dark green river, knowing the water temperature was probably a lot colder than the last time Charlie swam out to rescue a time traveler.

"I can do it." Thank God the team had invested in some cold water gear—neoprene suits, dive masks, and even snorkels. She was the stronger swimmer of the two, but it would take time to don the suit and prep for a rescue, if necessary.

As they contemplated their next steps, they both witnessed a massive fireball burst through the low-hanging clouds and streak across the sky.

"Shit!" Angel scrambled outside without even putting on his coat.

The pod landed ten yards from shore in a massive explosion of water.

"I'll suit up," Charlie said, heading for the back of the

Landcruiser. She grabbed a suit, stripped down to her under-wear, and prepped for a swim.

Angel had scooped up a stack of blankets and was halfway to the brand new dock that had been built since their last trip here.

Although at first he'd been hesitant in his role as official 'greeter' to the couple of arrivals they'd met in the few months since their new mission began, the experience had proven quite positive. The startled look on people's faces as they exited the disintegrating pods was quickly replaced by fear when Charlie and Angel approached with towels, dry clothes, a bottle of water, and some food. He would launch into his short introduction about who he was, what time they were in, and how their team was there to help.

Orr had described it to Charlie and Angel like a witness protection program. "We are going to help travelers who are lost create a new identity, find a place to live, find a job, and make sure to connect them with other travelers."

She zipped up her suit and charged down the rugged slope to the beach. The pod door had already opened, and a figure was attempting to navigate her next steps with cold water lapping at the edge of the doorway.

"Wait!" Angel yelled at the person who emerged. "Let us help you."

The figure's head snapped up, as if suddenly aware she wasn't alone.

"Quick, I think I might've spooked her."

Charlie joined him at the end of the dock. "I'm on it." She dove into the water with a life vest and swam quickly to the sinking pod. The suit protected her well from the cold water, but when the freezing water hit her face, it reminded her of the risk she was taking. With powerful strokes, she reached the pod in no time. Her unusual strength and endurance, likely created in her DNA by Allwood, didn't bother her anymore. Instead, she relished the thought of being able to help people who'd been damaged by the same man with the skillset he'd created in her. A full circle of sorts.

A middle-aged woman wearing a roughly-made dress stood in the open doorway, her bare feet exposed to the cold water rushing into the pod. *"Dov'è sono? Chi sei?"* She had long brown hair threaded with gray and milky blue eyes full of fear. "Who are you?" As she clung to the edge of the doorway, the soft organic material broke off in her hand. She gasped.

"You don't have much time before it disintegrates." Charlie treaded water and handed her the orange life vest. "Put this on, and then I can help you to shore. My colleague is waiting for us."

The woman shifted her gaze to the dock where Angel stood with his hands in his pockets and his hair lifting in the breeze.

"We can reunite you with other travelers, if you'd like." Anything to coax the worried-looking woman out of the sinking pod. "Please, take the vest."

Her pale eyes snapped to life. "Others?"

"Yes."

The woman snatched the life vest and slipped it on. Charlie talked her through snapping the plastic buckles and tightening the straps. As the new arrival pulled the second strap tight, the pod heaved to one side causing her to fall into the water. She screamed.

Charlie swam for her, knowing the shock of the cold

water must be terrible. The faster she could maneuver the woman to shore, the better. Angel had blankets waiting, then they could load her into the Landcruiser and blast the heat before they launched into their welcome message and the steps that would happen from there.

She grabbed hold of the inflated bladder that held the woman's head above water and managed to swim them both to the dock in record time. When they reached it, Angel lent a hand to help them both up the metal stairs at one end.

As the woman came out of the water, Angel gave an incredulous stare. "Risa?"

Charlie's brow wrinkled.

The woman scanned him from head to foot. "How can this be?" she asked in a shaky voice. "How can you be here? Am I dreaming?"

"Dearest sister!" Angel gathered her in his arms, unbothered by the cold water that dripped off of her, and hugged her hard.

"How is it possible?" Her whole body shook.

Charlie unfolded one of the wool army blankets Angel had brought from his vehicle and rested it across Risa's shoulders. "We need to move her into the Landcruiser. It's freezing out here."

Charlie had never seen Angel shed a single tear until now. After everything he'd been through, after the realization he may never see his sister again, after knowing he'd never be able to return to his time or see his family and loved ones—he'd never cried when he explained everything to her. But as he held his younger sister close, he bawled. Years of repressed emotions poured out of him—every fear, every sense of loss, every moment of loneliness he'd suffered.

When a few minutes had passed, and both brother and sister managed to gather themselves, Charlie asked, "Would you like to see Armas?"

Risa's eyes teared up for a second time. "He's here?" Before she could collapse to the wooden boards beneath her feet, Angel held her up. "My God, he made it?"

He gripped his sister tightly. "Yes." His eyes shone. "You named him after Dad?"

Risa met her brother's gaze and nodded.

"Will he even recognize me?" She touched her wet hair that had turned mostly gray. "He was so small back then. So very very small."

"A boy will always remember his mother," Charlie said. "Come, let's take you somewhere warm and talk about your future with your son."

"My future." Risa pulled the blanket close around her body and smiled.

As Angel led his sister toward the road, Charlie held back. The sight of the two long-lost siblings walking together after having been separated by hundreds of years of time made her forget everything else. Who would have thought when she first joined NCIS-A all those months ago that she would end up in the most rewarding job a person could have —saving those lost in time and making a place for them? How many more travelers would they encounter in the coming years? Angel couldn't remember the number of pods he'd seen that day when he'd climbed inside one himself.

"Are you coming, Charlie?" Angel looked back at her. She'd never seen his face so relaxed, his body so loose. The weight of worry and guilt had been lifted.

She straightened her posture, and, in an unhurried fashion, walked to the end of the dock to join them. "Yes, I'm coming."

Behind her the last of the pod sank under the waves. Any evidence of Risa's arrival disappeared.

Onto the next rescue.

The End

[Join K.J. Gillenwater's newsletter and receive a free science fiction short story.](#)

IF YOU LIKED THIS BOOK...
TRY READING 'AUTOMATED'

AUTOMATED: Available only in the U.S. Kindle
Vella store!

When Eli visits Chicago in 2043, he is shocked to find his dead wife reborn as a robot. Replica humans are illegal to manufacture, so who would create such a thing and why? As he delves deeper into the mystery surrounding his wife's past, her secrets begin come to light. Who was she? The discoveries he makes will shatter his world and bring him face to face with an enemy he never knew he had.

Start reading now!
First three episodes are always free.

ABOUT THE AUTHOR

K. J. Gillenwater has a B.A. in English and Spanish from Valparaiso University and an M.A. in Latin American Studies from University of California, Santa Barbara. She worked as a Russian linguist in the U.S. Navy, spending time at the National Security Agency doing secret things. After six years of service, she ended up as a technical writer in the software industry. She has lived all over the U.S. and currently resides in Wyoming with her family where she runs her own business writing government proposals and squeezes in fiction writing when she can. In the winter she likes to ski and snowshoe; in the summer she likes to garden with her husband and take walks with her dog.

Visit K.J.'s website for more information about her writing, her books, and what's coming next. www.kjgillenwater.com.

If you enjoyed this book, K. J. Gillenwater is the author of multiple books, which are available in print and in eBook format at multiple vendors.

- The Genesis Machine Trilogy: Inception, Decryption, and Revelation
- Revenge Honeymoon
- Illegal

- Aurora's Gold
- The Ninth Curse
- The Little Black Box
- Acapulco Nights
- Blood Moon

Short Stories & Short Story Collections:

- Skyfall
- Nemesis
- The Man in 14C
- Charlie and the Zombie Factory